DOUBLE TROUBLE IN THE EVERGLADES

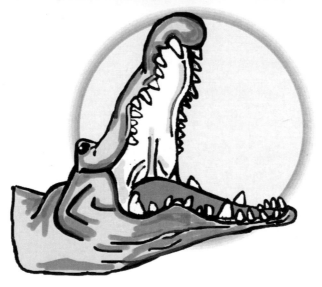

by Mary Morgan

Illustrated by Dawn McVay Baumer

© Buttonwood Press 2015
978-0-9965562-0-0

Enjoy a wild adventure-
Mary Morgan
2015

Manufactured by Color House Graphics, Inc., Grand Rapids, MI USA
July 2015

Published by Buttonwood Press, LLC
P.O. Box 716, Haslett, Michigan 48840
www.buttonwoodpress.com

Books by Mary Morgan

Published by Buttonwood Press, LLC

Stolen Treasures at Pictured Rocks

ISBN = 978-0-9823351-3-0

The Face at Mount Rushmore

ISBN = 978-0-9823351-7-8

Spies in Disguise at Gettysburg

ISBN = 978-0-9891462-2-7

Snow Den at Yellowstone

ISBN = 978-0-9891462-5-8

I WISH TO THANK

My husband Randy—the greatest source of encouragement.

My adult children, Shannon and Bryon, who remember our trip to Florida in a borrowed motorhome.

The Buttonwood Press team who makes this possible— Richard, Dawn, Marie, and Joyce.

Rangers Cory and Allison—out standing sources of information regarding Everglades National Park.

Brenda, John, Jennie, and Isaac for their technical edits.

Mary and Johnny Jacobs whose alligator adventure sparked a story.

Mary and Diane for their endorsements on the back cover.

DEDICATION

This book is dedicated to my grandchildren Makenna and Rennen Morgan who vacationed with me in Florida, and want to return. May they ever have the 'travel bug' to discover the natural wonders of America.

Chapter 1

"Three, two, one, go!" the ranger yelled, then blew his whistle.

In a blaze of speed, twenty-five teams of bikers took off as fast as they could, heading straight into the heart of Shark Valley.

"Ben, wait up!" his twin sister Bekka wailed from behind.

"What's the matter?" Ben called over his shoulder, being careful not to turn his bike into the front tire of the boy next to him.

"My helmet is crooked, I can't see."

Ben pulled over to the shoulder of the road and looked at Bekka who was stopped in the middle of the crowd. Kids with all colors and styles of bikes swerved so they didn't collide with her.

"Hurry! They're all getting ahead of us!" Ben said, looking up to the sky and groaning to himself. He wanted to be the leader of the group, not the tail end.

"Sorry," Bekka replied, pulling the strap of her helmet back into position under her chin. "I put my helmet on so fast, my ponytail made it go sideways. Let's go, we can catch them." At that, she put her feet back on the pedals and took off, leaving Ben behind.

"Hey!" Ben said, and stood up on his pedals to get more speed to catch his sister. "Keep going, don't slow down. The

ranger said there'd be a lot of animals out this morning. I don't want to miss seeing them."

"Or be the ones the mosquitoes can catch," his sister replied, looking down at her arms. "I've been bitten enough times to last me the rest of my life!"

"Me, too. Let's pass these kids if we can," Ben suggested as they got close to the back of some bikers.

"Left," Bekka called out, informing the group they were going to pass on the left. One by one, the bikers moved to the right side of the road so Ben and Bekka could pass safely on the left side of them.

"Thanks," Bekka called back to the bikers as they continued to move forward. The road was only one lane wide with swampy canals on each side. It wound through the middle of Everglades National Park in a big circle.

"That was easy," Ben said catching up to the next group of bikers. Some of the girls were laughing and pointing at a bird in the sky. Neither Ben nor Bekka looked at it. They were focused on passing them.

"Left," Bekka called out again. This group didn't move over as willingly as the other group. Some sped up faster and tried to stay ahead of the twins.

"Faster, Bekka," Ben said, his voice urging her to pick up the speed. Bekka pushed harder on the pedals and managed to pass six bikers.

"Dude, we have fifteen miles to go. We can't kill ourselves in the first mile," Bekka said, moving into the middle of the group.

"Okay, but I want to be ahead of everyone before we're done."

"But my legs are burning." Bekka's calf muscles were getting sore from pedaling so hard and fast.

Ben slowed down. His sister was right. They had plenty of time to get ahead of the other bikers. For now they'd stay with the group and then they'd find their chance to. . . .

"Duck, Ben! Duck!" Bekka screeched. Her eyes popped wide open.

"What the. . ."

Before Ben could put his arm up in front of his helmet, two long legs attached to the biggest bird he had ever seen flew right in front of him. He jumped off his bike before he fell over.

"What was that?" he asked, half-terrified, half-amazed. As he looked up to get a better look at the bird, his bike went off the road, over the bank, and into the canal.

"That, my friend," said a park ranger who ran over to check on Ben and help rescue the bike, "is a blue heron, one of the largest wading birds here in the Everglades."

"It freaked me out," Ben exclaimed. His heart pounded in his chest.

"Me, too" added Bekka. "I thought it was going to kick Ben in the head."

"I'm sure that wouldn't happen," the ranger replied. "They're used to taking off and landing in the water without wiping out our visitors. Here, let me help you get your bike."

"Are there alligators in that water?" Ben asked, keeping his eye on the bike sinking farther down into the water.

"Yes, alligators are all around here," the ranger answered. "In fact, one just walked behind the visitor center. We had to stop a man from trying to take a picture of himself with the alligator in the background."

"Wow!" Bekka exclaimed. "That could have been the last picture he ever took."

"That's for sure. You just can't be too careful," the ranger said as he stepped into the water. "People need to remember that a wild animal can't be trusted to not attack if they feel threatened."

"Hey, can I take your picture?" a photographer asked running up to Ben and the ranger who were bent over pulling on the bike. "I've been looking for something interesting to start writing about. This will make a great story in the magazine. You just made my day."

Ben's face turned red. That was the last thing he wanted to have written about him in *Twins for Life* magazine. He wanted to be known for his speed, for rescuing someone from drowning, or solving the next big crime to hit Everglades National Park. Why did a photographer happen to see him dunk his bike in an alligator-infested swamp? The next thing he knew, a video camera was in his face.

"What's your name, where are you from, and why do you think you were chosen to be in the Triathlon for Kids?"

Ben looked at the reporter and said the first thing that came to his head. "My name is Ben Cooper, I'm from Lansing, Michigan, and I guess I'm just lucky to be here."

Chapter 2

Actually Ben didn't know why he and Bekka were selected to go to Everglades National Park in Florida. His mom read a story in the December issue of *Twins for Life* magazine describing an adventure-of-a-lifetime offer for ten-year-old twins to be in a triathlon during Spring Break. She thought it would be a great experience for Ben and Bekka–as long as their father, a reporter for a Lansing newspaper, could go along. He would take pictures and write a story when they got home.

When Ben's mother told their family about the adventure, he asked, "What's a triathlon?"

"A triathlon is a sporting event where you do three things," she said, looking at the magazine article. "It says fifty lucky kids will be chosen to participate in a three-day event. They will canoe two miles to an Indian shell island, hike three miles in a swamp, and bike fifteen miles around Shark Valley."

"Do you win a prize?" Bekka asked. She and Ben liked winning prizes.

"Usually there are winners in a triathlon," their mother said, again looking at the magazine, "but not this time. The article says the purpose is to get young people outdoors to experience life in the Everglades."

"Coool," Bekka and Ben said together. They high-fived each other, grinned, and said, "Let's do it!" It was funny how often they said the same thing at the same time.

Bekka thought for a minute and said, "We know how to swim if we fall out of the canoe, we hiked five miles at camp last summer, and riding fifteen miles on a bike would be a piece of cake."

"Yeah, easy," Ben said, shaking his head. He and Bekka liked being outdoors and could handle all three things with no problem. "I think we should do it."

"Don't get your hopes up too high," Dad said. "I'm sure hundreds of other twins think they're lucky and will send in their names, too."

"But we're extra lucky," Bekka replied, smiling at Ben. Her eyes lit up like two candles. "It's about time we had another adventure."

"Oh, no, you don't," their mother said a little too quickly. "You two seem to get yourselves involved in things more often than most kids do in national parks, like discovering those men stealing things from sunken ships up at Pictured Rocks, and uncovering the plan of poachers at Yellowstone, and chasing down those guys at Mt. Rushmore. It scares me when you sniff out the bad guys. One of these times you'll find yourselves in too much danger. If you're chosen to go to the Everglades, I want you to promise me you won't go looking for trouble."

"What? Us go looking for trouble?" Ben replied, trying to keep from smiling. "We can't help it if we see things happening. Dad's a reporter, and you know, we have a nose for the news."

Hearing that, Dad broke out into a loud laugh. "What can I say? He's right. I think it's a great idea. You should send in their names. What other information do they need like who, what, when, where, and why?"

Mom rolled her eyes and then looked back at the magazine. "They need a picture of them together, our address, and their birth date."

The registration form to fill out was at the bottom of the page, so she wrote in the information: Ben and Bekka Cooper, 123 Penny Lane in Lansing, Michigan, ten years old, on October 11th. She cut it out of the magazine, found a picture of the twins celebrating their birthday with a number ten candle on their cake, put both items in an envelope, and mailed it the next morning.

Chapter 3

The month of January and half of February passed without the Cooper family hearing from *Twins for Life* magazine. Mom and Dad were convinced the twins were not among the lucky fifty chosen to be in the triathlon at Everglades National Park.

Ben and Bekka secretly hoped they would be chosen and maybe have a dangerous adventure. It seemed to be a habit when they went on vacations in national parks. They were clever and out-smarted the bad guys they met. Rangers were quite impressed with their keen eyes and quick thinking. For fifth graders, they did a great job.

One day as they waited to hear from the magazine, Ben and Bekka got out a large map of the United States to locate Florida. They spread it on the floor of Ben's bedroom. They found Florida and then looked to see where Everglades National Park was.

"Wow, it's all the way down at the bottom of Florida—at the ocean!" Ben said, surprised to see how far it was from Michigan. "It looks like a thousand miles away."

"I'll get my travel trivia book and see what it says," Bekka stated, heading for the bookshelf in her bedroom. She knew right where to find the book and opened it to the pages with information about Florida and its parks. Her eyes quickly spotted the paragraphs about Everglades National Park.

Bekka was famous for knowing important facts about places where their family had traveled and didn't hesitate to let everyone know what she knew. She called it FYI – *For Your Information*. Ben had to admit most of the time her facts were quite useful, so he didn't try to stop her from getting her book.

"Oh, my gosh! Mom is going to freak out," Bekka said, walking back into Ben's bedroom. "Listen to this. *Visitors in Everglades National Park may encounter the endangered Florida panther, bobcats, alligators, pelicans, crocodiles, python snakes, and much, much more.*" Her eyes got bigger with each one she listed.

"Sweet!" Ben said, imagining an alligator on one side of their canoe and a crocodile on the other. With the possibility of adventures like that, he really hoped they would be two of the lucky twins chosen to go!

"Bekka, Ben," their mother called with an excited voice. "Come quickly!"

Bekka put down her book as Ben jumped over the map. Fearing something awful happened they hurried to find their mother who was standing by their front door.

"What happened?" Bekka asked, hoping everything was okay.

"We've got mail," their mother said, waving a white envelope in the air. Her eyes danced with excitement.

"What is it?" Ben asked, jumping up to reach it.

Mom playfully hid it behind her back. "Guess who it's from."

"*Twins for Life*? *Twins for Life*?" Bekka asked, hopping up and down. Judging by the way their mother was acting, she just knew the letter had to be from the magazine.

"Seriously? Did we get a letter from *Twins for Life*?" asked Ben.

"We sure did!" replied their mother as she slit open the envelope. "We have to be prepared for disappointment if they tell us you were not chosen."

Bekka bounced up and down—very sure they had been chosen. Ben held his breath–waiting.

Chapter 4

Mom took a very long time reading the letter. Ben studied her face trying to tell whether or not they had been accepted. Bekka quit breathing for a whole minute and finally said, "Mom, this is killing me. Read faster."

A grin formed on their mother's face. She looked at Bekka, and then looked at Ben. "You made it! You're on the list of the fifty lucky twins chosen to spend Spring Break at Everglades National Park!"

Ben and Bekka grabbed each other by the arms, shook each other, jumped up and down, and let out a yell. It was going to be a trip of a lifetime—they just knew it. Panthers, and pythons, and pelicans, oh my!

"We gotta call Dad!" Bekka exclaimed. "He's not going to believe it!"

Ben ran to the calendar to count the days until Spring Break while Bekka called their father. Newspaper reporters sat near their telephones waiting for new news to be reported. He answered after the second ring.

"Dad, you aren't going to believe it!" Bekka yelled into the phone. "We're going to the Everglades… yes, we got a letter…no, I'm not kidding. Ben is counting how many days until Spring Break."

Bekka talked and listened and answered her father's questions as fast as she could talk. Her heart was beating almost out of her chest. She couldn't remember the last time she was this excited. She just knew *Twins for Life* magazine was not going to be disappointed that they had chosen her and Ben to go.

"Yes, I already read about it in my trivia book," she answered her father. "There are panthers, alligators, pythons, and crocodiles down there."

"What?" asked their mother in a very high-pitched voice, filled with alarm. "They didn't mention *that* in the article. They said you would be canoeing, hiking, and biking. I thought it would be safe and fun, not filled with danger. Who do I call to cancel your trip?" she asked scanning the letter for a phone number.

"Mom," Ben replied, "we're not going to get eaten by an alligator or chased by a panther. Bekka's book says panther sightings are rare. We'll be just fine."

"Yeah, Mom, they wouldn't put *us* on the endangered list," Bekka said, smirking. She thought she was being quite clever and funny since they had been studying endangered animals in school. But it didn't calm down her mother.

"That settles it then. I'm going with you and taking a first-aid kit–with snakebite repellent or whatever it's called. And I bet the mosquitoes are big enough to carry you out to sea. I heard Florida has big ones. I'm putting in a gallon of bug spray, too!"

Ben and Bekka just looked at each other. How embarrassing! They just knew the other forty-eight twins were going to laugh their heads off when they saw the Coopers arrive with an over-sized suitcase of first-aid supplies.

"Ben, how many days until Spring Break?" Mom asked.

"Forty-three."

"Good," Mom said. "I'll have time to learn how to suck venom out of a snakebite."

"Ew-w-w!" Bekka groaned. "That's gross!" She put her finger part way in her mouth acting like she was going to gag.

"Well, you never know," their mother said. "It might be useful. Hopefully, you'll only see nice things like flamingos standing on one leg or manatees swimming calmly past your canoe, not hearing you ran for your life from a wild animal. Are you sure you still want to go? It's not too late to back out."

"We want to go, we really want to go," Bekka said. "Right, Ben?"

"Oh, yeah!" Ben agreed, high-fiving his sister again. His imagination was already out in the swamp looking up at a limb where a snake hung above his head. If that really happened, it would be an adventure they'd remember for a long time!

For the next forty-three days until they left for Florida, Ben and Bekka worked out to get into shape. Even if they couldn't win a prize, they wanted to do well in the triathlon. With snow remaining

on the ground in Lansing, the twins went to the YMCA to swim and jog around a track. Their mother took a first aid class and learned how to care for snakebites. And packed lots of first-aid supplies. Finally the day to leave arrived.

Chapter 5

"Ben, wake up," his father said, shaking Ben's arm. "We just landed in Florida."

"Already?" Ben raised his head from where it leaned against the window frame and opened his eyes slowly.

"You slept through most of the flight."

"Wow, I can't believe we're here already." Ben closed his eyes and leaned against the headrest. He was still tired. Their family had gotten up early to finish packing and get to the airport on time. Their mother checked and rechecked everyone's suitcases to be sure nothing important was left behind, including half of the medicine cabinet.

Ben had been assigned a window seat on the plane so as they flew, he used his binoculars to look at the rivers and mountains far below. After a half hour, they flew into the clouds. It felt like they were in a cotton ball factory. Since he couldn't see through the clouds, he put down his binoculars and within minutes, he was asleep.

Bekka was too excited to sleep. Ever since she learned they were going, she couldn't think of much else. Her teacher at school caught her day-dreaming, looking out the window watching winter turn into spring. The days were getting longer and warmer. She

couldn't wait to be where it was warm, and they could swim and ride bicycles.

She had laid out her suitcase two weeks early, and packed and repacked her clothes. She couldn't imagine wearing shorts in March, but the ranger told them it would be warm. They had to be prepared for mosquitoes, so she packed long pants, too. They bought new sneakers, since they would use their old ones while wading knee-deep in swamp water. That sounded a bit creepy, but if it was part of the triathlon, Bekka could handle it.

On the airplane, she spent most of her time looking at her travel book. Everglades National Park was like no place they had ever been. There were hundreds of species of birds. Some would be migrating back north after spending the winter in warmer weather. She learned the difference between alligators and crocodiles and how to not run into a manatee with a canoe. She almost jumped out of her skin when she read that they could flip over a canoe if startled.

She was so excited, butterflies fluttered in her stomach. Secretly she hoped an alligator would come near them, but not too close. Just close enough to take a picture. She felt her jacket pocket to see if her camera was still there. It was and she smiled thinking of all the animals she hoped to get in a picture.

Bekka was getting famous for the pictures she took, especially on their vacations in national parks. Some of them helped rangers solve mysteries that were happening. If she hadn't had her camera at Mount Rushmore, the bad guys would never have been caught. Nor would the Snow Joes at Yellowstone.

Maybe, just maybe, she would be a famous photographer someday. She hoped they would have exciting things to take pictures of in the Everglades.

The pilot shut off the plane and thanked everyone for flying with them to Florida. Passengers stood up to get their luggage.

"Grab your carryon bags and follow me," Dad said as the four of them stepped into the aisle to leave the airplane. A long line of people with suitcases in hand stood behind them. It seemed everyone was in a hurry to get off the plane and get out into the Florida sunshine.

"Bekka, do you have your camera?" Mom asked starting down the aisle. She remembered seeing Bekka take pictures out the window.

"Yep. It's right here in my pocket," Bekka answered, feeling it once again in her jacket.

"Ben, do you have your binoculars? You were using them before you fell asleep."

"Oh, my gosh! I left them in the pouch in front of my seat," Ben said, turning around to go back. But he couldn't move. His path was blocked by passengers pulling their suitcases. The aisle was too narrow for even a kid to pass by.

"Just step in front of this seat," Mom said, pointing to the row of seats next to her. "We'll wait until everyone has passed by. Then go back."

Ben's face got red with people looking at him. He moved into the nearest row and sat down to wait.

"I can't believe you forgot your binoculars again," Bekka said, scowling and looking him right in the eyes.

She was reminding him of the time he forgot his binoculars in Mount Rushmore's movie theater and had to go back for them. But it was a good thing because that's when he overheard the plot of two men to blow up dynamite, and the bad guys didn't get away with their plans.

As soon as the aisle cleared, Ben dashed back and reached into the pocket in front of his seat. His binoculars had fallen to the bottom out of sight. No wonder he had forgotten them. He took one last look out the window. Palm trees were blowing in the wind and a flock of the largest birds he had ever seen flew by. As much as he didn't want to, he'd ask Bekka to look in her trivia book and find out what they were. That book could be annoying at times, but it had lots of answers.

Chapter 6

Out on the highway in their rented van, Ben started to get excited. They were just a few miles from Everglades National Park. Best of all, after months of snow and cold, soon he would be in shorts, camping, and sleeping near a lake with alligators. He could hardly wait.

"Dad, can I go into the store and pick out my sleeping bag?" asked Bekka. The letter from *Twins for Life* said camping gear would be at the campsites, but everyone had to bring sleeping bags. They didn't have room in their suitcases to pack theirs, so it was decided they would buy four new sleeping bags and donate them when they were ready to return home.

"Yes, Bekka. Everyone can choose their favorite color so we can tell them apart," Dad replied, looking at her in the rearview mirror. "We'll have a large tent with plenty of room for our luggage and sleeping bags."

"And the first aid kit," Mom added. Dad smiled and shook his head. Both were hopeful they would not have to use any of it. He parked the van in a spot near the door of the camping gear store and they all went inside.

"I want that purple one," Bekka told the salesman. Someone had created a huge pyramid of sleeping bags in the center of the store, and she chose one near the top.

"I want this one," Ben said, struggling to pull a blue sleeping bag from the bottom of the pile.

"Ben, no! Stop! Don't pull on it. They'll all fall over!" The words were barely out of his mother's mouth, when a huge stack of sleeping bags fell forward knocking over a basket full of balls.

"I didn't see that coming," Ben said chasing after a half dozen balls. "That wasn't supposed to happen. I'm sorry, sorry, sorry." Every time he picked up a ball he said sorry one more time. He threw the balls in the basket and started restacking the sleeping bags. Bekka chased a ball heading for the exit door.

"Now that all the sleeping bags are on the floor, do you even see the blue one you wanted?" Bekka asked. She was sure most other brothers would have chosen one closer to the top. Ben scowled at her and picked up the closest blue sleeping bag. How embarrassing!

"Where are you camping?" asked the salesman.

"In Everglades National Park," replied Ben. "Bekka and I were chosen to do the Kids Triathlon this week."

"Is that the twin event we've been hearing about?" asked another clerk. "Sounds like kids from across the country are coming. Are you two twins? You look kind of alike, but not identical."

"Yes," Bekka said, grinning from ear to ear. She and Ben were almost the same height. He was in a growing spurt, their mother said, so he was just about an inch taller. Their hair was the

same sandy blond color and their eyes were both blue. Ben liked short hair, but Bekka liked hers long, making it easy to put it in a ponytail.

"Sometimes I might not want to admit he's my brother–like when he knocks down a pyramid of sleeping bags," Bekka said, "but usually he's okay." Ben nudged her with his sleeping bag.

"You'd rather have me for a brother than Luke, right?" Ben asked, knowing for sure Bekka would choose him over their neighbor any day.

"You got that right!" his sister said, high fiving him. Some of the guys in their neighborhood were–well, she couldn't even come up with a word to describe them.

"I hope you're the outdoor type. Ever been in a canoe before? Do you ride bikes? Ever wade in water above your knees?" the sleeping bag salesman asked. "If you answered no, then you've got quite a surprise coming. Are you afraid of snakes or gators?"

"Snakes and gators?" questioned their mom, raising an eyebrow as she jerked her head in his direction. "I *hope* they don't cross our path."

The two clerks looked at each other and laughed. One of them responded, "Actually, if you leave them alone, they'll leave you alone. We just like to see the reaction of visitors when we mention them. We hope you have a good time. Just watch out for eyeballs watching you."

At that the two clerks laughed, and the Coopers left the store, each carrying his own sleeping bag. Two others left the store right after the Coopers. They had seen and heard it all.

"Those kids just might cross our path," one said to the other as they climbed into their Jeep. "They don't seem to be from around here and won't know what we're looking for."

"Good," replied the other.

Chapter 7

Upon arriving at the entrance gate at Everglades National Park, the Coopers were instructed to park their van and be at the flagpole at five o'clock where a ranger would meet and greet everyone.

"We got here just in time," Dad said, pulling the van into a parking space. "With five minutes to spare."

Ben and Bekka hopped out and stretched their legs. They had been cooped up most of the day, and it felt good to be outside.

Bekka spun in a circle, with her arms stretched out and her face lifted toward the sun. It was almost sixty degrees warmer than when they left Michigan three hours ago. "I think we should stay a whole month!"

"Yeah," Ben said slowly, amazed at the different kinds of trees that surrounded them. There were evergreen pine trees, palm trees and some he didn't recognize. Some had stringy moss hanging down with large blue-feathered birds sitting near the top. Suddenly three of them flew away. "Look at those birds. I saw some like them when we were getting off the plane. They're huge! What are they?"

"They're probably blue herons, one of the largest birds in the Everglades," Bekka informed him. Ben half smiled. He knew she would know.

"Let's go," Mom said, putting on her sun hat. A park ranger with his hat in his hand walked out of the visitor center and headed toward the flagpole.

"Race ya," Bekka challenged Ben, and took off. In a flash he caught up to her and together they reached the grassy area around the flagpole at the same time. Bekka just needed a small headstart to keep up or beat Ben. His longer legs could beat her in a race if she didn't.

A large group of twins and their parents joined them. Some twins were so identical you couldn't tell them apart. Others only looked similar to each other. Parents began introducing themselves and soon most of the twins were, too. Ben and Bekka weren't shy. Within just a few minutes, they met several other sets of twins. It was surprising to learn how far some had traveled.

Ranger Cory started his welcome speech and within a minute, a twelve foot reptile came up out of the canal and walked toward the visitor center, distracting most of the crowd.

"Ben, look! There's an alligator!" Bekka exclaimed, poking her brother in the arm. Ben jumped in surprise.

"Whoa, a real live gator. He's walking around like we aren't even here."

The ranger stopped speaking when he saw several heads turn to watch the alligator cross the road and head for the grass behind the visitor center.

"It didn't take long for one of our pet alligators to show up and welcome you," Ranger Cory said. "He's probably looking for a good spot to sun himself. Or he's heard you twins are dangerous and wants to keep his distance from you." A giggle rippled throughout the crowd as the ranger smiled and looked back to his audience.

"You have alligators for pets?" Ben asked, not quite believing what he heard.

"Well, not actually, but they do hang around here as if they were our pets. We like to say they come out to welcome you to Everglades National Park."

"Do they ever attack people?" asked a boy named Rennen.

"We haven't had any reports of alligator attacks for a long time," replied the ranger, "but you must remember, they are wild and you need to treat them that way. You are not to feed them, don't go near them, and keep a safe distance of twenty feet if you feel the need to take a picture of one. There are thousands of them in the park, so always keep your eyes open for them."

Quite a few adults raised their eyebrows in surprise while most of the twins stared at the alligator. It seemed so strange to see it walking around. "Okay, where did I leave off?" the ranger

said, looking at his clipboard. He reached for a box on a nearby table. Opening it, he pulled out a lanyard and held it up.

"Here are your identification tags–they have your name and state on them as well as a color code. Please hang them around your neck and wear them at all times. I *need* you to wear them. With so many twins, I'm seeing double. How do you parents tell them apart?" he asked, looking at some of the kids. They positively looked just alike!

A couple of girls with red hair and freckles burst out laughing. It happened to them all the time. Their grandpa still couldn't tell them apart.

"Okay, next item," Ranger Cory said. His clipboard had a long list on it. "Your campsite location. Many of our campgrounds don't have running water or bathrooms. That's called dry camping."

Most of the mothers looked at him in surprise. Camping without a bathroom? No way!

"We selected Monument Lake campground at Big Cypress Preserve. It has bathrooms and showers." That brought on many cheers.

"Wait, it gets better. Knowing alligators like to sun themselves in grassy areas, your tents are located in the back row of the campsite away from the lake. We wouldn't want you to unzip your tent and find an alligator sleeping nearby."

"Seriously?" called out one mother.

"It happens," the ranger replied.

Most of the boys were okay with alligators in the campground, and Bekka thought an alligator sleeping by their tent would make a great picture. But others did not.

The ranger was almost done with his instructions. "Your family's name will be on a post next to your tent. Unload your sleeping bags and luggage and meet at the campfire area at six o'clock for a hot dog roast. Later, when it gets dark, we'll have s'mores and gaze at the galaxy."

"What?" asked Ben.

"We'll look at the stars," Bekka informed him. "Get it, gazing at the galaxy? Since most national parks are away from cities with bright lights, you can see a million more stars."

"Oh yeah, makes sense," her brother said, swatting a mosquito which had just landed on his arm. "These bugs are bad."

"They sure are," Bekka agreed, scratching at a fresh bite.

"If no one has any more questions, please come get your packet of information, and we'll see you at six o'clock for dinner," the ranger said.

One by one, families got their packets and headed for the campground to find their tent.

Chapter 8

Following a map of the campsites, the Coopers located their tent in Row C. It took only a few minutes to unload their luggage and sleeping bags and spread out their things.

It felt good to be camping again, but sleeping on the ground might be difficult. Usually the Coopers traveled with their camper which had comfortable beds, but they decided for a few nights, they could sleep on the ground–as long as alligators stayed away. Dad looked at the distance to the lake and agreed with the ranger that it was safer for those sleeping in tents to be farthest away from the lake. Just before they headed for the picnic area for dinner, Bekka zipped the tent shut to keep mosquitoes out. She hated hearing them buzz by her head when she was trying to fall asleep.

"Look at all these people," Bekka said, looking at the crowd gathering around the picnic tables.

Rangers pointed to the hot dogs and skewers for people to cook them on over the blazing campfire. Ben and Bekka knew how to do it, but others needed some instructions. For some, this was the first time they had ever been camping. Within minutes, the smell of roasted hot dogs filled the air. Everyone cooked theirs just the way they liked them and then sat down at picnic tables to eat.

"I'm so starved, I could eat six hot dogs," Ben said as he wrapped his hands around a bun oozing with ketchup.

"It seems everyone eats more when they eat outdoors," Mom replied, squeezing mustard onto her hotdog. "I know I do."

After a few minutes a ranger blew his whistle.

"You can roast another hot dog if you want one. We have plenty," he said, looking at the extra hotdogs sitting on a tray. Before he could say another word, he swatted his ear and ducked like he was being attacked.

"If you haven't noticed already, you'll find our mosquitoes are hungry this spring. Spray yourself often with repellent. Keep your tents zipped shut and turn off your flashlights when you go in and out at night. There's nothing like the buzzing of a mosquito by your ear when you're trying to sleep".

"You've got that right," a father called out. Many laughed while some scratched new bites.

"About eight o'clock in the morning," the ranger said when it got quiet, "breakfast will be served at these picnic tables. Twins, eat plenty of food because the triathlon begins at nine o'clock, and there's nothing to eat on the trail." He stopped talking and handed a large box to another ranger.

"My assistant has a packet for each of you to open. Inside you will see a map of the Everglades and the locations for the three events. There is also a copy of our Junior Ranger booklet. A Junior Ranger is someone your age that helps us keep our park looking just the way you see it–full of birds and animals with exciting places to explore." He waited until every family had one and then said, "Go ahead and open them."

Sounds of envelopes being ripped were heard as curious twins and their parents opened the packets and pulled out a booklet.

"On the cover of the booklet, you'll see a scavenger hunt. That's part of our triathlon. In addition to biking, hiking, and canoeing, see how many of these sixteen birds, animals, insects, and plants you can get pictures of. There's a prize for those who find them all."

Ben and Bekka liked that kind of a challenge. They were competitive and liked winning prizes.

"Hey, I already saw a heron and a mosquito," Ben stated, looking at the pictures. "And an alligator," he said rather proudly. "I'm almost half way there!"

"But we didn't get pictures of them," Bekka reminded him.

"Oh, yeah. Well, there's always tomorrow. Bekka, keep your camera handy. I want to be in the picture with some of these reptiles."

The ranger gave them time to quiet down and explained what was to come. "The first event in our triathlon is a bike ride around Shark Valley."

"Shark Valley. Are there sharks there?" asked Makenna, a girl sitting next to Bekka.

"No," chuckled the ranger. "Almost everything but sharks. It's named for the Shark River that runs through the park. There's a fifteen-mile road where you'll see all kinds of wildlife. Possibly you'll catch sight of a bobcat running through the grass. For sure, you'll encounter alligators—just leave them alone. Most of the time they are sunning themselves. Watch for anhingas. They are big wading birds with an unusual shape to their wings. Get a picture of one if you can. The favorite of many visitors is the flamingo. It used to be there were lots of them here in the Everglades, but not anymore. If you see one, then this is your lucky day."

"Oh, no, I want to see flamingos," Ben and Bekka's mother said quietly. "Not panthers or pythons."

"Parents," Ranger Cory said to the adults, "you'll ride in the open air tram bus to the observation tower and watch for your twins to pass by. The tower is sixty-five feet high, so you can see for miles. Have your cameras ready. The view is fantastic. Twins, make sure you have your cameras and binoculars with you. You'll

see things in the water and in the sky that will amaze you. Even though it's a triathlon, it isn't a race. You're here to enjoy nature. Keep your eyes and ears open–there's a lot going on here in the Everglades. Any questions?"

Half-way back in the crowd, one hand went up.

Chapter 9

"If you're on a bike and there's an alligator on the road, what do you do?" asked Bekka. She wanted to go all fifteen miles, but not if there was an alligator on the road.

"Because alligator attacks are so rare, we suggest you go around the tail end—but at a safe distance. Remember, don't make them feel threatened. We haven't had an alligator attack for a long time, so let's keep it that way. Oh yes, if you see a baby alligator on a large lily pad, stay back. Its mother is nearby watching you. Don't get too close. She will attack you if she thinks you might hurt her baby."

Bekka shuddered thinking about it. She remembered how large the alligator was at the visitor center. She wasn't about to become alligator bait.

The ranger looked around to see if other hands were raised. Not seeing any, he said, "Okay, let's have some s'mores. Soon it'll be dark enough for you to enjoy our night sky. It's amazing how much brighter the stars appear here. Keep track of what constellations you identify and let me know. Make a new friend while you make a s'more. Don't be shy, who wants to be first in line?"

The ranger ripped open a bag of marshmallows while another ranger opened the graham crackers and chocolate bars onto a large tray on the table.

"Woohoo!" Ben exclaimed, running for a skewer and a couple of marshmallows. It had been months since he had had a s'more, and he couldn't wait any longer.

It looked like a feeding frenzy of hungry sharks. Everyone crowded around the table to get their treats. Skewers with two and three marshmallows were pointed into the campfire. Some people cooked them until they were golden brown while others let them burn until they were black. Gooey marshmallows stuck to fingers and lips while the melted chocolate bars oozed out of the graham crackers.

Everyone enjoyed every bite. Many parents who hadn't had a s'more since they were kids went back for a second one.

"Mmmmm, so good!" a boy named Caden said, smiling with a wide grin. Chocolate covered his teeth. He and his brother Camden were from Iowa and had never flown in an airplane before. Their grandpa Price had come with them and held a video camera up to Caden's face.

"Hi, Mom!" Caden yelled into the camera. He looked disgusting.

"Gross," Bekka said and rolled her eyes. Makenna agreed with her. "Why do boys do that?"

"What?" Ben asked. He thought it was funny.

What he did not think was funny were the number of mosquitoes landing on him. He ran for the bug spray and then decided to take cover. At this point, he didn't care what stars were out. He headed for their tent!

Chapter 10

"Hey, sleepy-head, wake up!" Ben heard his father say and then felt a hand shake him. He was sleeping so soundly, even the noise of birds honking overhead didn't wake him. "Rise and shine. Bekka's been up for half an hour and breakfast is almost ready."

At the mention of food, Ben jolted awake. The last thing he wanted was to miss a meal. The smell of fried bacon and blueberry pancakes filled their tent. He bolted out of his sleeping bag and grabbed his clothes. Within two minutes he was out of the tent.

"That didn't take long," his mother said, surprised at his speed.

Ben looked around. The sun was shining through the mist hanging over the lake. It was kind of cool but a little creepy.

Ben hadn't ever seen anything like that before. His imagination ran wild wondering if the world's largest alligator would surface at any moment– its big black eyes looking right at him. I gotta quit watching those alligator hunting shows on TV; it's got me spooked, he told himself.

Turning, he headed for a table full of boys who were ready to dig into the pile of pancakes and bacon. And dig in they did. Hardly anyone said a word as they ate. A table filled with girls was the opposite. They talked more than they ate. Wearing nametags

helped them get to know each other faster, and soon they were chatting about their favorite movies!

Half-way through breakfast, Ranger Cory pulled up in his truck. He walked toward the tables with a clipboard in his hand. With his other hand, he swatted at a mosquito that had landed on his neck.

"Good morning, everyone," he said, looking around at the group. "You look well fed. Everybody ready for adventure?"

"Yes!" many kids yelled back.

"Good. The weather is perfect for a fifteen-mile bike ride around Shark Valley. You should see lots of animals today. Don't forget your water bottles, cameras, and bug spray. Meet me at the rental shop at the visitor center in Shark Valley in half an hour to get your bicycle and helmet. Parents, coffee and donuts will be served at the observation tower. We're expecting a great day. Any questions?"

The ranger looked around for a raised hand and waited for someone to speak up.

"Oh, yes, I almost forgot. Bring your binoculars. They're a tool of discovery for nature lovers here in Florida. You'll see things you've never seen before. Any questions?'

Once again he looked around for anyone raising their hand, but no one did.

"Okay, if everyone knows what to bring and where to go, then let's head out!"

Cheers, loud enough to wake anyone still sleeping, were heard all over the campground. Twins and parents ran to their tents to get what they needed and soon headed for their vehicles.

While he waited outside for his sister to pack her bag, Ben looked around the campground through his binoculars. They were just about the last ones still at their tent.

"Let's go, Bekka."

"I'm coming, I'm coming!"

Bekka took an extra minute to make sure she didn't forget anything important. Camera, batteries, water bottle, notepad and pencil, and bug spray. She tucked each item into her backpack and walked out. Ben zipped the tent shut. A pesky mosquito had buzzed around his head during the night until he buried himself inside his sleeping bag. He was determined to keep out any new ones.

"Thanks for being on bug patrol, Ben," said his mother who was loading their first-aid kit into the van. "If anything bigger than a mosquito gets you today, I'm prepared."

"Even an alligator?" Bekka asked as she climbed into her seat.

"I'll just wrestle it, like they do on TV," her mother replied, making a fist and showing her arm muscles.

"I want to see that one," Dad said. "Bekka, have your camera ready."

"It is," Bekka said as her father started the van and headed for the campground exit.

Twenty-five vans and cars left the campground in a caravan. A few minutes later, two men climbed into a jeep. They were about to set their plan in motion.

Chapter 11

An hour later, few bikes remained in the rental shop after all the twins had chosen their favorite style or color. Ben and Bekka had matching blue and silver ten-speed bikes. Everyone waited by the side of the building until the ranger blew his whistle.

"One last warning to watch for wildlife on the road, stay hydrated, practice bicycle safety, and we'll see you at the end of your ride. But first, it's time for a group picture by the flagpole."

Protests erupted. "Do we have to? I don't like my picture taken." Bekka rolled her eyes, wondering why boys protest so often.

To the surprise of everyone, three photographers with huge cameras were by the flagpole.

"*Twins for Life* magazine sent photographers to cover the triathlon," the ranger explained. "They want action shots and your comments during interviews. Give them lots to write about."

All of a sudden, the boys wanted to be in the picture. Bekka laughed at their willingness to pose for the photographers. They wanted to be in a magazine.

Makenna and Rennen moved their green and white bikes over next to Ben and Bekka. Green and white were their school colors so it was an easy choice for them. Makenna was a little short for her age while Rennen was as tall as Ben, but they rode

the same-size bikes. With so many twins to get in one picture, a photographer told the boys to make a second row behind the girls. That made it work.

Ranger Cory went to the end of the second row with the boys. Bekka gave her camera to her father to take a picture of the whole group. He planned to use it when he wrote about their trip for the Lansing newspaper. Makenna and Rennen lived in Williamston, not too far from Lansing, so their names would also be included in the story.

After the pictures were taken, parents and grandparents headed for the tram which would drive them to the observation tower. They were excited about the birds and animals they might see. Mrs. Cooper hoped a flock of flamingos would fly in while her husband looked for bobcats running through the tall grass.

Just as the ranger was about to give the 'three, two, one' countdown for the bikers to start, Bekka took off her helmet to put her camera strap around her neck. She clipped her helmet strap together, but her ponytail got stuck sideways, causing the helmet to cover her left eye. She had to fix it to be able to see, and that's how they got so far behind at the beginning of the bike ride.

Rushing to get ahead of the other riders had not been a good idea. It was then Ben lost control of his bike after the blue heron flew inches over his head. Hopping off just in time, he watched his bike roll down the bank and into the swamp, sinking toward the bottom. It was a good thing a ranger came along to help Ben who didn't know the danger lurking not ten feet away.

And that's when the reporter from *Twins for Life* stuck a video camera in Ben's face asking for his name, where he was from, and why he was lucky to be chosen to come.

Maybe Ben wasn't lucky after all, Bekka thought, seeing his bike in the swamp. But this wasn't the right moment to mention it. She took one picture of him and the bike, and then another. Someday Ben would laugh about it, but not now. He wanted to be one of the first ones to cross the finish line, but it wasn't going to happen. Good thing this wasn't a race!

"Watch your hand," the ranger warned Ben. "That's sawgrass."

"What's sawgrass?" Ben asked, jerking his hand out of the water. It looked like ordinary tall swamp grass.

"See the sawtooth edges? They're razor sharp. You can rub the grass from the bottom up without a problem, but if you rub it from the top down, it'll cut you. That's why we wear long pants."

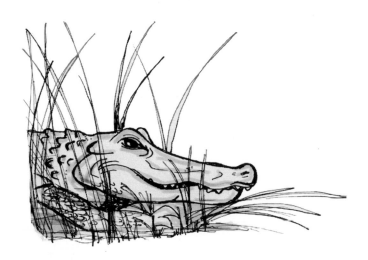

Ben jumped back farther and let the ranger pull on his bike. He didn't want to use his mother's first-aid kit on the first day.

The water moved and then Ben saw an alligator watching them. He jumped back even more when he saw the baby alligator on the bank in the sun. No wonder the mother kept her eyes on Ben and the ranger. Ben heard the click of the photographer's camera. He hoped the man was getting good pictures.

As they pushed his bike back up the bank of the canal onto the road Ben said, "Thanks for being a rescue ranger."

"You're welcome. Glad I was here to help and possibly save you from trouble. Just watch out for low flying birds. Egrets, herons, and ibis swoop in when they see apple snails in the mud. They'll peck around until they don't find any more and then move on to other areas. Sorry one scared you. I hope nothing else happens today."

"Me, too!" Ben said and took off on his bike.

Riding next to him, Bekka asked, "You know how you said you wanted to be in pictures with reptiles? Wait till you see the one I got of you and that alligator."

"You were the one taking pictures? I thought it was the man from the magazine."

"He got a couple and then went to find someone else to talk to," Bekka replied. "He didn't see the alligator in the canal."

Ben was disappointed he wasn't in a dramatic picture, but hoped his bike rolling into the canal would be mentioned in the article.

"Stop!" Bekka yelled, and pulled her bike to the side of the road.

"Now, what?" Ben asked, turning around.

Chapter 12

"You made us stop to get a picture of a dragonfly! A dragonfly!" Ben said, totally annoyed.

Taking a picture of a dragonfly sitting on a cattail was nothing! If it had been a panther, a python, or a bobcat, then it would have been okay, but not a measly dragonfly.

"But it's on the list of things to find," Bekka replied, remembering the things listed on the scavenger hunt.

She had her camera in hand and was ready to get the picture when a bird that had been soaring above them suddenly swooped down right behind them. Bekka jumped and grabbed Ben's arm.

"It's a snail kite," she said, whispering. As the bird neared the ground, it snatched something from the water's edge and flew back into the air.

Ben ducked, but Bekka tried getting it in a picture. "Nobody's going to believe we saw one."

"And no one's going to believe we were dive-bombed two times by birds," her brother stated. "What kind of a kite did you say that was?"

"It's a snail kite and it's rare. FYI–it's really a hawk, but it only eats apple snails, or snails that look like apples, so they call it a snail kite."

"Wait a minute. I'm confused," Ben admitted. "Apple snails are snails that look like apples. But snail kites are really hawks that eat apple snails. Some names just don't make sense."

"Yep, you got it," Bekka said, nodding her head. She closed her camera, totally forgetting the dragonfly, which had flown away when Ben ducked.

"Any other snails I have to be concerned about?" Ben asked.

"No, except the people at the finish line are probably gonna say we pedaled as fast as snails. We are so behind," Bekka said.

"Come on, let's see if there's anybody we can pass," Ben said, taking off again.

After five more minutes, they saw the observation tower. There was nothing to see for miles except tall grasses standing in a foot of water. While waiting for the twins to finally go by, their mother got her wish and saw two flamingos strut by. Their father didn't see a bobcat but was fascinated with a flock of anhingas. They had to be the strangest looking birds in the universe.

"There they are! There they are!" Ben and Bekka heard their mother yell as they got closer to the observation tower. Their parents had been quite worried when all the other bikes had passed by.

"Hi Mom! Hi Dad!" both kids yelled together. They waved as their father took a picture.

"Where have you been?" their mother called to them. "Do you need any band-aids?"

"No, but you won't believe what happened. We'll tell you all about it later," Ben yelled as they pedaled past the tower. They were having fun just the two of them.

A moment later, a man with a big backpack whizzed by, scaring Bekka. She almost fell into the canal. "He didn't even yell, left."

Two minutes later, a ranger rode by going just as fast, looking like he was chasing the other man. Or maybe he was in a hurry to help someone.

"Wow, I wonder what happened. Let's pedal faster to see if someone fell off his bike," Ben said and stood up on his pedals to increase his speed. Bekka was right behind him.

For the rest of the fifteen miles, they didn't see anyone down on the ground. But when they arrived at the finish line, two rangers were talking to the man who had passed them so quickly. They were looking in his backpack.

"Makes you wonder what's going on," Ben said quietly to his sister as they went by. "There must be trouble in the Everglades."

"Wait a minute," Bekka said looking above the heads of the men. "Palm tree. We need a picture of a palm tree. Let's take it here, and if two rangers and a suspicious man just happen to be next to it, good for us."

Without being detected, Bekka snapped the picture and eased her camera back into its case. That's how a good detective did it.

Chapter 13

Around picnic tables later that night, the kids talked faster than mosquitoes could bite. Each one had an adventure and each one wanted to talk. Most had never ridden fifteen miles. None had ever ridden where there were alligators, snakes, and the possibility of seeing a Florida panther.

The ranger had them break up into groups according to the color on their name tags. Ben, Bekka, Caden, Camden, Makenna, Rennen, and two other brothers, Tomas and José, were together.

Not knowing a better way to select who should go first, the ranger told them to go in alphabetical order–telling what they saw, heard, and experienced. The nametags helped with that.

Since her name started with B, Bekka took a breath to start talking. "Let's see, what should I mention first?" she said, tapping her cheek with a finger.

"Did you fall off your bike?" Tomas asked, trying to help her get started. Little did he know she was bursting inside to tell it all.

"No, I didn't–but *he* did," she said, pointing to Ben. "We got off to a slow start, but were catching up when Ben freaked out and jumped off his bike because a huge bird flew within an inch of his head. His bike went into the canal and had to be pulled out by a ranger."

All heads turned toward Ben who started to protest. "I couldn't help it. Let me tell it. All she did was take pictures." Everyone sat totally silent listening to them talk.

Bekka continued her side of the story, "When Ben's bike sank to the bottom of the swamp, a ranger and a magazine reporter saw it happen and came over. The ranger went down for the bike and the reporter put a video camera in Ben's face. He had to tell why he was lucky to be there. Personally, I think his luck ran out because just then an alligator swam over near his bike. I kept taking pictures even after the reporter left."

Bekka stopped to take a breath. Everyone sat with their eyes wide open. Mr. and Mrs. Cooper hadn't heard any of this and were just as surprised as the other twins.

Ben picked up the story from there. "But you got freaked out when that hawk flew behind you." Ben tried to keep the snail names straight, but in the end, everyone got confused and started laughing. Neither Ben nor Bekka mentioned the man on the bike or the picture Bekka took by the palm tree in case they shouldn't have.

Caden and Camden, José and Tomas, and Makenna and Rennen relived their adventures, but none were as adventurous as Ben and Bekka's.

Caden and Camden had to stop quickly when an alligator came up from the canal and crossed the road. They remembered what the ranger said and rode around the tail to be safe.

Tomas had a flat tire, so he and José waited ten minutes for a ranger to come fix it. They had a bet as to who would be faster– the ranger getting there or the turtle crossing the road. José thought the turtle won by a hair. The ranger laughed.

Makenna and Rennen reported that they were among the first ones to finish the ride. A photographer was there to get a picture. Ben was jealous.

"Let's stay together and do things as a group," Rennen suggested. He liked adventure and the Cooper twins seemed to make it happen. Each one hoped the hike through the swamp would be eventful.

They didn't have a clue.

Chapter 14

"Today you will slog through the slough," Ranger Cory announced the next morning after breakfast.

"Say what?" someone asked. People couldn't believe what they just heard.

"You heard correctly, it's called slogging through the slough."

Mr. Cooper chuckled to himself. He had read they would be slogging in the slough, but he didn't know slough was pronounced slew. He thought it was pronounced like tough. He shook his head. It was another exception to a spelling rule.

The ranger continued his instructions. "For three miles, you'll be trudging through muddy, algae-filled water learning about cypress trees and the wildlife that calls the water its home. I hope you read in your instructions to bring tie-up tennis shoes and long pants. Tie-up shoes will stay on your feet in mucky water, and long pants will protect your skin from getting cut by sawgrass."

Ben looked down at his bare legs. Warm weather or not, it was time to go back to the tent for his jeans. Looking around, he could tell others were thinking the same thing.

"Did any of you notice or touch the rough seagrass yesterday on your bike ride through Shark Valley?" Ranger Cory asked. Many hands went up.

"The word 'Everglades' means 'river of grass'. There are several kinds of seagrasses in this fifty-mile-wide river which is less than a foot deep in most places. Ever wonder where the salt water of the ocean meets the fresh water of rivers running toward the ocean? It happens right here in the Everglades."

A lot of kids and parents had puzzled looks on their faces. It did make them wonder where the salt water ended and fresh water started.

"The water in the Everglades is a mixture of salt and fresh called brackish water. Today's part of the triathlon will be in Big Cypress Preserve which is fresh water. Tomorrow's canoe trip will be in salt water. For today, besides your camera, binoculars, and bug spray, you'll want a change of clothes and shoes, and your polarized sunglasses, which will help you see deeper into the water and protect your eyes from the sun's harmful rays. Any questions?"

Once again, the ranger looked around and waited to see if anyone raised his hand for more information.

"It looks like you know what is needed, so I'll meet you at the visitor center at Big Cypress Preserve in a half hour."

Everyone scrambled back to their tents to get their things and to change into long pants. The sun was climbing farther into the sky and the temperature was rising.

"Hey, Ben," Rennen yelled from the entrance of his tent. "You and Bekka still want to stick together as a group?"

"Sure, if you want to," Ben answered.

Rennen and Makenna seemed like they might be fun to do things with, although Makenna looked like a girly-girl with her hair fixed with those headbands. He hoped she didn't scream at spiders. That would really be annoying.

Caden and Camden and Tomas and José were walking back from the bathhouse with toothbrushes in hand and saw Ben and Rennen talking.

"Hey, guys," Rennen yelled. "Wanna slog with us?"

"Sure, why not?" answered Tomas. Just as he stepped into his tent, a blood curdling scream came from a tent in row B.

"A snake, a snake!" a girl yelled. Heads popped out of many tents. Everyone wondered where the snake was at. A number of men headed toward the tent where a mother was hugging her daughter.

"A snake crawled past our tent!" the girl cried. "I didn't know there were going to be snakes by our tents."

"We're in the Everglades, surrounded by water," one of the men reminded her. "Snakes are going to be here, but the ranger said if you don't bother them, they won't bother you."

It didn't help. The girl still freaked out.

Chapter 15

A half hour later, while parents enjoyed free time, a ranger talked to the twins about the Big Cypress Preserve Cypress. When he was finished they divided into teams. Along with their new friends, Ben and Bekka were on Team Anhinga. Standing at the edge of the knee-deep water, some almost changed their minds. It was beyond anything they expected. The water was warm, but it was dark brown, and with each step Ben was sure he would lose his shoe in the mucky bottom.

Each group had been assigned a ranger to guide them, but the ranger for the Anhinga team left to get first-aid for a photographer who had been taking their group's picture and lost his balance. As he fell, he forgot about the danger of grabbing sawgrass and cut his hand quite badly.

"If our mother was here," Ben told the group, "she'd have enough band-aids for all those cuts."

The ranger told their group he would send another ranger to guide them. In the meantime, they were to look up, look down, look all around for secrets of the slough.

Standing in the water, smooth-bark cypress trees surrounded them. They had a shape Ben had never seen before. Branches were growing in all directions. He couldn't imagine wandering through there at night. The moon would make such creepy

shadows, he was sure he could walk on water if that was the only way to get out!

"Bekka, you doing okay?" Ben asked, feeling a bit uneasy. The water was above their knees and walking was difficult. At times he felt he should protect his sister, even though she said she didn't need protecting.

"I'm okay," she replied. "You okay?"

"Yeah."

"What is it we're supposed to be looking for?" Caden, the boy from Iowa, asked as he pushed his polarized sunglasses back up his nose. They kept falling down because of the greasy sun screen.

"We're supposed to find a cypress tree with a knee," his brother, Camden answered.

"Oh yeah, that's right." Caden was so focused on not falling down in the water he forgot what the ranger had told them to get a picture of. "But what's a tree knee?"

Tomas and José laughed. They didn't know either.

"FYI," Bekka announced, "each of these trees have knees. See that part that is raised up? That's a knee. And those roots? They are out of the water because they need to breathe air just like the bark does. And look, there's an air plant growing on the side of the tree."

"Tree knees, air plants. How do you know this stuff?" Makenna asked, quite impressed Bekka knew so much tree trivia.

"I have a book. I'll show it to you when we get back to the campground." She looked at Ben and smiled a big toothy grin.

Sometimes he wished he knew the stuff his sister knew, then he could impress people, but that would mean he'd have to have his nose in a book all the time. That wasn't for him. But if they ever invented a slough-slogging video game with snakes crawling in and out of cypress trees, he'd buy it in a heartbeat and become Ben the Snake Slayer of the Slough!

"Ben, did you hear Caden?" Bekka asked her brother who was so deep in thought he didn't hear Caden ask to borrow his binoculars.

"What?" Ben asked, looking at her.

"He wants to use your binoculars," Bekka informed him.

"Oh, okay," Ben said, pulling the strap from around his neck. "What are you looking at?"

"There's a huge bird in that tree over there, and I want to get a better look," Caden explained, putting the binoculars up to his eyes. He clunked them against his sunglasses. "Ow, that hurt."

"That's an anhinga, I think," Bekka said.

"It's got really weird-looking wings and a long skinny neck," Caden commented. The ranger was right—Ben's binoculars were a tool of discovery for nature lovers. It brought everything far away up close.

The black anhinga was fascinating to look at, but another movement in the binoculars caught Caden's eye.

"Sh-h, everyone, there's a snake hanging in that tree," Caden said, trying to keep his voice calm.

"Where?" Rennen asked, putting his hand up to Caden's face. He wanted to look through the binoculars, but Caden wasn't giving them up.

Caden pointed to a nearby tree and continued to stare. Everyone looked for the snake until they saw it draped over a limb. It slithered higher, its green tongue flicking in and out–probably in search of insects.

"He sees us!" Makenna squealed. "Look! He's looking at us. I think he's gonna come get us. Let's get out of here."

Her voice was getting higher and squeakier with every word. She grabbed so tightly to Bekka's arm that it hurt. No one could move or take their eyes off the snake. They didn't want it to get into the water without them knowing it.

Bekka opened her mouth to let out one of her famous screams. Ben couldn't let that happen. The whole swamp would be terrified. He had to take charge.

Chapter 16

"Caden, I need my binoculars back," Ben said as he reached for the strap. Caden handed them back, but didn't take his eyes off the snake. He watched its every move.

Looking into the binoculars, Ben guessed the snake was five or six feet long. It was hard to tell exactly how long it was since it was wrapped around a branch. But it was multicolored and had fangs. It seemed to flick its tongue at them.

Bekka shuddered. Makenna let go of her arm. Bekka decided to get one picture of the creepy thing, trying to remain calm as she lifted up her camera. She was sure when their mother saw the picture, she would not remain calm.

"Let's go this way," Ben said, hearing voices of other sloggers not too far away. Makenna and Bekka held hands–keeping each other from running away. There was just something about snakes that made them want to lose control.

"Remain calm and stay together," Ben instructed, leading the others forward in water that was still over their knees.

"How do you know there aren't snakes everywhere?" asked Makenna. Her eyes looked left and right as fast as she could make them move.

"Hey, here comes a man," Bekka said, glad to see an adult. "Let's see if he's a ranger and ask if we can stay with him. Rangers

know poisonous snakes from the others." They all moved in the man's direction.

"Excuse us," Ben said as they got closer. "Are you a ranger? We were wondering if you could tell us how to tell which snakes are poisonous and which ones aren't."

"Ah, no, not actually," said the startled man. He wasn't expecting the kids to ask him questions.

"We saw one in that tree over there," Ben said, pointing to a tall one behind the man.

"I don't know anything about any snake," he said not looking up at the tree.

The man recognized the kids so kept his head down hoping his ball cap and sunglasses would keep them from recognizing him. He stuffed a bag inside his shirt, turned his head away from them, and began to slog fast in the opposite direction.

"That was rude," Bekka stated, scowling at the back of the man's head. "He could have been a bit friendlier." Dealing with the man helped her forget about the snake.

"There's an island over there," Rennen said. "Let's check it out." His adventuresome spirit wanted to explore it.

"That's not an island. They call it a hardwood hammock," Tomas said.

"A what?" asked his brother José.

"A hardwood hammock. It's like an island raised up above the level of the swamp, with trees growing on it. That's where the liguus tree snail spends the dry season."

"Oh, no, not another Bekka," Ben groaned, totally surprised to hear an explanation like that. Tomas smiled. He was the quiet type that remembered things he read and heard.

"Don't you remember the ranger talking about the liguus snail?" Tomas asked Ben.

"I guess so," Ben admitted, "but I must have forgotten what he said. Lig-whatever it is, didn't stick in my head. Yesterday it was snail kites and snail bites. I'm so confused."

Makenna giggled. She thought Ben was funny.

"Ben, just remember snail kites eat apple snails," Bekka reminded him.

"Whatever. If I see one of them on a tree, I'm calling it liggy, for short," Ben said as they reached the island. "Here liggy, liggy."

"Seeing anything interesting in the slough?" a ranger asked as she walked out from behind a tree on the hammock.

Everyone jumped at the sound of a voice, causing the kids to bump into each other like dominoes. Makenna caught her brother Rennen just before he fell over into the swamp.

Chapter 17

"You scared us!" Rennen exclaimed, holding his chest.

"Sorry about that. Your ranger had to stay with the photographer who got cut, so they sent me to walk with your group. My name is Allison." She looked at the kids and then at their nametags. "Got any good pictures?" she asked spying Bekka's camera around her neck.

"Yeah! I just got one of a huge snake in a tree back there. It freaked us out!" Bekka exclaimed and shuddered again. "How can you stand being out here with snakes like that?"

"I've been a ranger here for ten years, and I'm getting used to it. Out here we're surrounded by gumbo limbo, wild tamarind, poison wood, and pigeon plum."

The kids looked around thinking they were going to be attacked by island aliens. Their eyes were as big as quarters.

"Sounds a bit scary, doesn't it?" Ranger Allison asked. "But, not to worry, they are friendly trees who wouldn't hurt a flea."

"Or a tree snail?" Ben asked.

"Wow, I'm impressed. Someone even knows there are tree snails," Ranger Allison remarked.

Ben had a cocky smile, but no one said anything. They knew the truth about Ben and snails.

"Anybody know what's so special about tree snails?" the ranger asked.

In his quiet way, Caden raised his hand. "They hibernate on trees."

"Somebody's done his homework," the ranger said, giving him a high-five. "Want to check them out?"

"Yeah!" they all said.

She took two steps to her right. "This is a Gumbo Limbo tree." The girls giggled as she said it.

"Weird name," Ben whispered under his breath, his right eyebrow raised a half inch. Gumbo Limbo he thought to himself. *Where do they come up with these names?*

"It's a smooth bark tree—the perfect location for a snail to spend the winter which is our dry season. In fact, there's one right over here," she said, walking to a nearby tree.

Much to their surprise, hanging on the tree trunk was a brightly-colored hard shell of a snail. It was about two inches long and looked like it was glued in place.

"Coool," three of the boys said together. No one had ever seen anything like it. Everyone leaned in to get a better look. Camden reached up to touch it, but the ranger's hand stopped him.

"A tree snail isn't just an ordinary snail," she explained. "Look at the cool colors in each stripe. Believe it or not, more than fifty color combinations like blue, peach and tan, or orange, green, and brown have been spotted on snails here in the Everglades."

"Why do they hibernate?" Bekka asked, looking very closely at it.

"Snails depend on water to stay alive, so during the dry winter months when it doesn't rain, they attach themselves to a tree and stay there till it rains again. In the summertime, it rains every afternoon, so there's no shortage of water."

"What keeps them from falling off when they're hibernating?" asked Makenna. She checked the under-side of the shell to see what was holding it onto the tree.

"Well, you tell me. What do you see?"

They looked closer to investigate what kind of glue it used. No one had a guess.

"The snail is able to spread a layer of white mucous on the bark which is like glue that holds it right in place."

The boys looked closer at the shell and then at each other. It looked like a magic trick.

"It's really weird how it can stay up there all that time," Ben remarked, looking around at other trees. "Are there anymore?"

The ranger was quick to point to other Gumbo Limbo trees. "There sure are. Walk around the hammock and notice the color combinations on the shells. Make sure you take pictures. You don't get to see these very often."

Naturally, Bekka volunteered to take pictures of every snail on the whole island. The group split up to find as many as they could.

"Bekka—over here," Makenna called out. "Here's a pink and orange and brown one."

"This one has blue and green and tan," reported Rennen from a different spot. Bekka went running over to his tree.

It didn't take long until they found more than a dozen shells with different color combinations. No two were alike.

"Hey, you guys, here's a white ring where a snail used to be," Tomas said. In an instant, everyone was there looking at the spot on the tree.

"Where's a white ring?" asked Ranger Allison, quickly coming over to them. She gasped when she saw the snail was missing.

"What? What happened to the snail?" She looked on the ground to see if she could spot the shell lying at their feet.

The kids could tell something was wrong, or she would not be so upset.

Chapter 18

"Here's another white ring," José said, pointing to an empty spot on the backside of another tree. Ranger Allison hurried over and gasped at another white ring where a snail once hung.

"What's wrong?" asked Bekka, thinking the ranger was overreacting.

"There was a snail here, but it's gone. Until about twenty years ago, it was legal for people to snatch them off trees and sell them for quite a lot of money. But now it's different. You can't take anything out of a national park. These snails are protected and can't be removed. Someone just did this. It was here half an hour ago when I showed them to another group. Those two snails were here. Someone stole them!"

"Do people take them just to have them, like in a collection?" asked Rennen who had quite an impressive collection of dinosaurs. He thought maybe people collected snail shells for their aquarium. The colors would look sweet underwater.

"The main reason people take them is that they get a lot of money for them. The bad thing is, now the snails will shrivel up and die." Hearing that made the girls feel sad.

"Aw," said Makenna, the world's biggest animal lover.

"Did you guys see anyone that wasn't a part of your *Twins for Life* group?" the ranger asked.

"Yes," Ben stated. "Just before we got here to this island, I mean hammock, a man was walking kind of fast with a bag in his hand."

The ranger looked directly at him. Her eyebrows shot halfway up her forehead. "What did he look like? What kind of a bag did he have? Did he say anything to you kids?"

Ranger Allison could hardly stop asking questions. It upset her to think someone had stolen the snail shells when she wasn't looking.

"At first we didn't know if he was a ranger," Bekka answered, looking around at the other kids. She was trying to remember exactly what happened. "We wanted to know if he could tell poisonous snakes from other kinds. He told us he didn't know."

"He had a bag of something," Tomas added. "It was camouflage."

"Yeah, you're right it was camouflage," added Caden, who suddenly remembered what the bag looked like.

"How big was it? Did it look like he had big or small things in it?" Ranger Allison asked.

"Well," Camden said, "it was like a small bag from a store. Maybe just the right size for carrying shells. When Bekka started talking to him, he put it inside his shirt."

"I thought he didn't want it to get wet," Bekka said. "Maybe he didn't want us to see he was carrying something. Maybe he was hiding the shells." Her detective brain was getting fired up!

"There's a penalty for stealing snail shells or anything else from a national park," the ranger informed them. Turning to Bekka, she asked, "Any chance you got a picture of him?"

"No, but we could tell you what he looks like."

"Okay, describe him. About how tall was he?" Allison looked at Ben. "Was he taller than your dad?"

"No, I think they're about the same." Ben kind of guessed.

"He had brown hair and a dark blue shirt," Tomas added.

"Did he wear glasses? Did you get a good look at his face?"

"No," Ben replied, "because just before he got near us, he turned his head away like he didn't want to talk to us."

"He went past those cypress trees out there," Bekka pointed behind her. "And that's the last we saw of him."

"Would you kids mind talking to the head ranger when we get back and tell him everything you just told me?"

"Sure," Ben said, looking around at the others who were nodding their heads yes. They couldn't believe what was happening. They were in the middle of a crime scene.

"Something happened at Shark Valley yesterday," the ranger started to say and then quit. The expression on her fact told them she had said more than she should have.

Bekka tried to get more information out of her. "What happened?" She didn't let on that she and Ben saw the man with the two rangers.

"I can't say. It's just upsetting when people do things they shouldn't in the Everglades. It messes with the ecosystem."

"Ecosystem, what's that?" asked Rennen.

"It has to do with nature and how everything here in the Everglades exists. One thing depends on another. See those cypress trees? Their leaves drop into the water. The leaves decay and small fish eat them. Larger fish eat the smaller fish, and so on. It's a food chain. Did you see any wading birds pecking at the ground yesterday?"

"Yes," Makenna said, remembering how she stared at some with curved beaks that were more than a foot long. "I never saw birds with beaks like that."

"They were probably roseate spoonbills. Their long beaks allow them to peck for food on the ground or in the canals," Ranger Allison replied. As she talked, she looked around for anyone hiding behind trees.

Then she added, "I just can't understand why people come into the park planning to steal or harm something. If you can help us sketch the man's face, it might help other rangers be on the lookout for him. Hopefully, he won't take any more tree snails. We don't have that many left. There is one thing we have a lot of."

"What's that?" asked Ben, not knowing he was about to get one of the biggest surprises of his trip.

Chapter 19

Reaching down into the water, Ranger Allison scooped up a handful of green algae that was floating on the surface and squished it into a ball. "Sometimes kids do this."

Without warning, she threw the ball of glob at Ben!

"What the?" he exclaimed. "I've been slimed!" Along with everyone else, he looked down at the green blob of icky algae on his shirt.

The ranger started laughing. "Up north, you have snowball fights. Down here kids have algae glob fights. Rangers usually don't do this, but I couldn't help myself. It's a stress reliever."

Ben picked some algae, squeezed it into a ball, and threw it at Rennen, who threw some at Caden. The girls giggled their heads off watching as each boy got slimed. They jumped out of the way as the yucky stuff hit the water and splashed onto their clothes. It looked like green sponges were flying everywhere. Then Ben turned and threw some at the girls.

"Why, you slime ball!" Makenna yelled, picking up some algae. She hurled it back at Ben.

"Yeah, slime ball," Bekka said, letting a handful fly toward her brother. She turned her head sideways knowing more was coming her way.

Their screams and laughter were so loud other groups came to see what was going on. No one joined them, but someone took their picture.

"Look, there's an alligator," Ranger Allison yelled to the kids, who were covered with green slimy goo. It was the only thing she could say that would distract them and get them to stop.

Hearing her words, the kids dropped their algae and turned to look in the direction she pointed. With the mud and algae stirred up, it was surprising anyone could see into the water at all.

"Are there really alligators here?" asked Tomas. He was having fun with the algae fight, but searched for bulging eyes in the water.

"Well, to tell you the truth. . ." the ranger started to answer. Her eyes got really big. She turned her head from side to side looking each person in the eyes. "If I say yes, will you want to stay out here much longer?"

"No way!" admitted Makenna and Bekka together.

"Did you know they have two sets of eyelids?" the ranger asked. The kids shook their heads no and looked around to see if an alligator was watching them. "They use them like goggles to see underwater."

"Like they can be under there right now and we wouldn't know it?" asked Makenna. She was ready to be done with this science experiment.

"Don't look now, but you're being watched from that tree," Allison said, pointing to a row of cypress trees. "It's an Eastern Indigo snake, one of the endangered species. If you don't bother it, it shouldn't bother you."

"I'm out of here!" Camden said. He'd seen enough.

"Me, too!" agreed his brother Caden.

"Me, three!" Tomas declared.

"Me, four!" stated Makenna and Bekka at the same time.

"Wait a minute, I want to see it in my binoculars," Ben said, putting them back up to his eyes. "Wow! It's big! And it's coming down the tree."

"It might be a good idea for us to wade over to that shore," Allison said, hurrying the group along.

Not taking time to turn around, Bekka held her camera backwards and took a picture. The snake was about to enter the water. But it wasn't the only thing in the picture.

Chapter 20

Shocked to see her twins looking like jolly green giants at their slogging adventure, Mrs. Cooper couldn't help but ask, "What happened to you?"

"What?" Ben asked, looking down at his drenched clothes caked in green slime. A glob was still in his hair and some splatters were dried on his face. He did look like a jolly green giant.

"Were you attacked by sea creatures from the deep?" Never had she seen them look so filthy.

"We had a blast!" Ben stated. "You wouldn't believe it! The ranger hit me with a ball of green algae slime, so I threw a ball of it at Rennen, and then everybody was doin' it. Even the girls. The ranger said kids do it all the time."

"But you stink! You surely can't get into a rented car with those clothes on. They'll make us buy the car before sunset!"

Ben and Bekka burst out laughing. That was the funniest thing they had ever heard their mother say.

They were still laughing when Ranger Allison came over to where they were standing. "Your children made my day. I'm impressed with how much they know about the slough. And Ben seems to know so much about snails. He was such a good sport when I hit him with the ball of algae."

Ben raised his head up a bit higher and Bekka gave him a good poke in the arm. If it hadn't been for her, he still wouldn't know the difference between apple snails and snail kites. Or a snail bite!

"Most of all," Ranger Allison ended by saying, "I want to thank them for giving me a helpful description of someone who possibly stole some liguus snails off trees in the hammock."

Mrs. Cooper's jaw dropped and her eyes popped when she heard the twins were involved with a thief. They hadn't mentioned that yet.

She tilted her head, looked at the twins and then asked the ranger, "What's going on? My children seem to be drawn to mysterious happenings no matter which park we're visiting."

"Mom, it's okay. We aren't in any danger–yet," Ben stated. His words did not help her relax.

"Yet? What do you mean yet?"

"Let me explain," Ranger Allison cut in. "During the winter months, which is our dry season, liguus snails attach themselves to smooth bark trees until we get more rain. They have very colorful shells and are quite valuable to shell collectors, so people come here to the Everglades for the purpose of removing them from the trees."

"Mom, you should have seen them," Bekka said excitedly. "They have pink, green, blue, and other color stripes on them,

and they were stuck to the tree with—like white glue. What's it called?" she asked the ranger.

"It's a ring of white mucous which stays on the trees when a snail is ripped off," the ranger explained.

"And you were involved, how?" the twins' mother asked again, putting her fingers on the side of her forehead. She did that when she was puzzled.

"Well, we weren't actually involved, except we saw a man in the water carrying a bag and, when he saw us, he hid it inside his shirt," Ben said, using his hands to demonstrate.

"We didn't know anything happened until we discovered more white rings on the trees. And that's when she got all excited and had us describe the man we saw." Ben hoped his mother understood what he was saying.

Ranger Allison nodded her head as she listened to Ben and then turned to Mrs. Cooper. "So, I would appreciate it if you would give permission for your children to tell our head ranger what they remember. They might be quite helpful in our search for this man."

"Sure, they can go with you," Mrs. Cooper said without hesitation, "as long as no bad guys leave a message at our campsite saying they know who we are, and we should mind our own business. That happened once and it almost made us go homc right then."

Ben and Bekka grinned remembering how one morning up at Pictured Rocks they found a message stuck to a hot dog skewer on their picnic table. Their mother was terrified, but they weren't. They were sure they could catch the bad guys at their own game.

Later that evening sitting inside their zipped-up tent, the Cooper twins talked about this new mystery. How could they catch a sinister snail snatcher? What was he going to do with the snail shells and how did he think he could get away without getting caught?

Bekka turned on her camera to look at the pictures. What she saw made her jaw drop. She showed one to Ben who exclaimed, "It looks like there is trouble in the Everglades. Are you thinking what I'm thinking?"

"Yeah," she said. It was too late for them to do anything about it. It was dark and the nighttime sounds of the Everglades surrounded their tent. They crawled into their sleeping bags wondering why once again they were involved in a mysterious happening. Maybe their mother was right—they were a magnet for trouble. They couldn't wait to see what would tomorrow bring.

Chapter 21

"Dad, make Bekka promise she'll sit still even if an alligator swims next to our canoe," Ben begged the next morning as they drove to the Gulf Coast Visitor Center. It was the day for the third part of the triathlon—padding a canoe around the islands on the west coast of Everglades National Park.

"Where we're going, it's manatees you have to watch out for," their father said, looking at Ben in the rearview mirror. "I'm sure we'll be just fine. Right, Bekka?"

"Right," Bekka replied. "Ben worries too much."

"What?" Ben shot back.

Bekka didn't like it when Ben thought she couldn't handle scary situations. She'd show him.

They crossed the bridge out to the island where the visitor center was located. They saw a sign welcoming them to the Ten Thousand Islands in the Gulf of Mexico.

"Ten Thousand Islands. Are we going to canoe around all ten thousand islands?" Ben asked.

"Hardly," Bekka replied, looking up from reading. "My book says it takes eight days to canoe from here all the way down to the farthest part called Flamingo."

"Flamingo, that's where Mom should go if she wants to see flamingos," Ben suggested.

"Well, actually, the ranger told us there aren't many flamingos there anymore. Most of them are over at Shark Valley where they find more food to eat," Dad informed Ben as he pulled into a parking space and shut off the van. "Grab your things and let's go. This is what I've been looking forward to." Since canoes hold only three people, only one parent was allowed to go. Their dad volunteered to do it. He wanted to see reptiles in their natural habitat.

Inside the building, Ben walked over to a huge wall chart that showed many of the fish and sea creatures that live in the Ten Thousand Islands. *So much to explore in so little time*, he thought. He was excited about this canoe trip. He just couldn't be sure Bekka wouldn't freak out if an alligator or a manatee swam past them.

"Where are we going?" he asked his father, who was standing by a wall map. His dad showed him several routes outlined with a red marker. Everglades National Park was bigger than either of them ever imagined. Several boys were looking at the map and said the same thing.

A ranger entered the room and asked for everyone's attention. He shook his head, blinked his eyes and smiled. Everyone knew what was on his mind.

"Welcome, everyone, to the third day of our triathlon. I think I need my eyes examined because I keep seeing double." He

stopped talking as little by little the crowd snickered about him seeing so many look-alike twins.

"We hope you've had fun exploring our park. Our goal for the triathlon is for people to get outdoors and experience what is here. From what I've heard, some of you have had quite the adventures on your bikes and in the slough. Hopefully, you'll have just as much fun exploring our waterways."

Looking down at his list, the ranger read something and then said, "Eight canoes will go into the Ten Thousand Islands, eight canoes will head up the Turner River, and nine canoes will go to Sandfly Island. As I call out your name, please go out through that door to get your life jackets, paddles, and canoe."

Bekka looked around for Makenna and Rennen and their father. Something must have happened since they had been ready to leave the campground at the same time as everyone else. Bekka hoped their friends would be in the same group, so they could finish the triathlon together.

The ranger called the Coopers' name and pointed to the group going to Sandfly Island. Ben smiled as he headed outdoors. It was where he wanted to go.

Chapter 22

As Bekka waited in line to get her lifejacket, she watched five white egrets fly in and land near the canoes. Overhead, a big black bird circled and then dove into the water, bringing up a fish.

"Ben, did you see that?" she asked, poking his arm. "A bird just dove into the water and caught a fish!"

"No! Where?"

"Over there," Bekka said, pointing over to the right. "Watch, there's another just like it. I'm going to try to get a picture of it with a fish in its mouth."

Bekka turned on her camera, looked toward the sky and then followed it down to the water. But the bird was too fast and she missed getting the fish before the bird swallowed it. Instead, she took three pictures of a roseate spoonbill that landed near them. It seemed to strut as it walked around pecking the ground for insects. Their long curved beaks were amazing. It walked near her father, so she got a picture of it and him as he held their canoe paddles. He called to her and Ben, "Tell the man you need a medium size lifejacket."

"Bekka! Bekka!" she heard Makenna's voice call over to her. Bekka breathed a sigh of relief as Makenna and Rennen dashed toward them. Their father went over to get their canoe and paddles.

"What happened?" asked Bekka.

"Six alligators were in the middle of the road sunning themselves, and we couldn't go around. We had to wait until they got good and ready to move."

"You're kidding!" Bekka said. "They weren't there when we went by. Wow! You made it just in time. Stand by us. This is the line to get life jackets."

As the four of them waited, the boys watched as blue herons dove into the water, picking up fish and eating them as they flew. It was amazing to watch birds snatch fish like that out of the water. Bekka looked around at those who already had on their lifejackets.

She wondered if many had ever canoed before, or if this was their first time.

"Make sure you pull the straps snug after buckling them," the attendant told each person as she handed them their lifejacket. "If it's too loose, you could slip out of it if you fall into the water."

"Dude," Rennen said to Ben, "it's a good thing we know how to swim." Makenna gave her straps an extra tug since she was thinner than the others.

"All right, canoers," Ranger Cory said when it looked like everyone was ready. He blew a whistle to get everyone's attention. He was excited for them to see his favorite part of Everglades National Park.

"Is everybody ready for a great time of canoeing?" he asked.

"Yes!" came the loud reply, with lots of clapping and cheers. After being with the families for two and a half days, the ranger recognized some familiar faces. He noticed Ben and Bekka in the crowd and smiled. He appreciated the helpful description they had given of the man with the bag of snails. An artist drew a picture that looked very much like him.

"Let's review some important points," the ranger said. "You'll canoe two miles through the Chokoloskee Bay over to Sandfly Island where you'll see old Calusa Indian shell mounds. It's an historic site I think you'll find quite interesting." Heads turned in the direction he was pointing.

"Twins, who knows what a mangrove tunnel is?" the ranger asked, looking at the kids for an answer. Bekka knew, so raised her hand. He pointed at her.

"Mangroves are like viney trees that grow close together and cross over making like a tunnel."

"Right," the ranger said. "Here in the Everglades, mangrove trees form tunnels over the water. After you leave Sandfly Island this afternoon, you can paddle around other islands. You'll see the tunnels all along the waterway. They're low, so stay in your seat. Once in awhile you might have to lean backwards, but just keep paddling."

Kids started laughing as the ranger bent backward and moved his arms like he was paddling a canoe.

"Keep your camera and binoculars handy. Animals are more active in the morning, so you might see a bobcat swimming out in the Ten Thousand Islands, porpoises and dolphins might jump in the air. And oh, yes, a word of caution—you may encounter manatees. There's a speed limit, but it's for motorboats. Manatees can't swim fast enough to get out of the way of a speeding boat. I don't think any of you will be paddling fast enough to run one down, but please remain calm when you're around them. They've been known to flip over canoes when frightened by them."

Ben looked at Bekka who turned away. She wanted to stick her tongue out at him, but didn't. She was determined more than ever to not show any fear.

Chapter 23

Seeing some of the girls squirm at the mention of manatees over-turning canoes, the ranger went on to a new subject.

"As a treat, twins, you will paint and create an Indian mask to take home as a souvenir." He held up several masks that were on a display table.

"Cool," Rennen said to Ben. He liked art and painting things, and wanted to start working on his mask. He would hang it on his bedroom wall.

"After lunch, you can explore the other islands on your own. Just don't go too far as it's easy to get turned around. Remember, this is not a race. It's just a fun day on the waterway. One last thing—put on an extra layer of bug spray. The mosquitoes are threatening to carry us away today. Any questions?"

"Can we leave our sisters on the island?" one brother asked.

"No, but I do believe sisters can leave brothers there," the ranger replied, making everyone laugh.

"Woohoo!" Bekka yelled. Ben poked her, and they laughed together.

"Parents, please sit in the back of your canoes to steer it. Twins, one of you will sit in the middle seat while the other will sit in the front and paddle like crazy. You can trade places from time to time, but stay low and don't move at the same time. Wear your

life jacket at all times. Your life may depend on it. Oh yes, there are alligators. Don't feed them, don't go near them. Leave them alone, and they'll leave you alone."

Bekka's head snapped toward her father who looked at her and smiled. Ben just nodded his head up and down. He didn't have to say a word. Manatees and alligators were out there waiting for them.

Just before the canoes pushed off shore, a photographer came around taking pictures of the group and each family as they got into their canoes.

Ben had claimed the front seat and took a paddle from their father. He was the self-proclaimed commander of the ship!

"Smile," the photographer said, bending over to get a close-up. Ben gave him the biggest smile ever. He really hoped it would be in the magazine article. Bekka took a picture of the photographer taking their picture.

"Aren't you the ones who were slimed yesterday?" the man asked Ben and Bekka. They were surprised he remembered them.

"I got a good picture of you coming out of the slough. You were a mess. I'll be watching for you today. I hope you have something good for me to take a picture of." Ben hoped the one of them coated with slimy algae wasn't too embarrassing.

"Wait a minute," the man said remembering something. "Aren't you the kid whose bike went into the canal on the first day?"

"Yeah," Ben said as his face turned red. He hoped Bekka didn't open her big mouth and tell everyone around them what had happened.

"I'm glad I got your group rather than one of the others going out to the islands or up the river. You seem to be a great subject to take pictures of." The photographer laughed and moved on, taking pictures of other canoes.

"You seem to have quite a reputation, Ben" his father said. "Hopefully today you won't give him a third event to write about. I do believe you two are going to get mentioned in the magazine. How many copies should we buy? A hundred, maybe two hundred?"

"If it's embarrassing, none!" Ben declared.

Chapter 24

Ben was good at paddling the canoe. He felt like an explorer discovering new places. Bekka took pictures of every bird that flew overhead and every canoe that went by. The people were friendly and all said hi.

Because Ben made paddling a canoe look so easy, halfway across the Bay, Bekka decided she wanted to switch places and paddle.

"My turn to paddle, Ben," she declared. "I want to do it now."

Ben didn't want to stop. "Five more minutes, okay?"

"No, you've done it a long time. I'm tired of being in the middle. I want to paddle for awhile," Bekka said and stood up. The canoe wobbled back and forth.

"Bekka, be careful," their father warned. "Stay low when you stand up. Ben, lay the paddle down, turn around on your seat, and walk back very slowly. Too much motion will land us in the Bay."

Both kids moved slowly as they exchanged places. Their father held his breath thinking of the creatures on the wall chart that might be down below them.

Bekka sat down very carefully in the front seat and picked up the paddle. She put it into the water and immediately splashed Ben as she brought it back up.

"Aw, Bekka, you got me all wet!" he protested.

"Sorry." She was trying hard to paddle like Ben did, but the wind began blowing harder and their canoe started going in a circle. It tipped to the left and then to the right. Ben held onto the sides in terror.

"Bekka, put your paddle on the other side," her father instructed a few minutes later, wishing he could be at both ends of the canoe at the same time.

Bekka tried, but it didn't help. She put her paddle into the water on the left side, then on right, then left again, hardly touching the water. They either went in circles or headed for other canoes going by.

She wasn't the only one having trouble. Only a few minutes after they had taken off from the shore, a canoe crashed into them almost tipping them over. Bekka was so scared she screamed for five seconds. Ben was sure they could hear her all the way up to Disney World.

Ben was about to explode inside and finally said, "Bekka, put the paddle straight down in the water and pull backwards."

"I'm trying," she said, clamping her jaw shut and pushing down and pulling back as hard as she could.

"Dad, can I puh-leeze paddle?" Ben begged. "She's going to get us all killed."

"I am not!" Bekka declared, pushing the paddle farther into the water. It seemed to help them go faster. She was determined to make it to the island.

"Nice and smooth now, Bekka. Keep us in a straight line," her father said calmly, hoping she wouldn't give up. And she didn't.

"Look, there's a porta-potty at the dock," Bekka announced when they were almost to Sandfly Island. Ben let out a huge sigh of relief. He wanted to kiss the ground.

Chapter 25

A ranger waded out to help pull their canoe ashore. The smell of Indian tacos on fry bread greeted them as they walked up to a picnic area.

"Something smells so good," Ben said, looking around for the food table.

"Ben, are you still on a see-food diet?" his father asked.

"Oh, yeah, I see food and want to eat it." Ben answered. He was beyond hungry and was sure he could eat a platter full of whatever they were serving.

"Welcome to Sandfly Island," said a woman dressed in authentic Indian dress. "My ancestors were great fishermen for hundreds of years and created this shell mound. There is a boardwalk that goes straight across the island. If you walk it, you'll see the historical home of a family who were the last ones to live here."

Ben listened and swatted at three mosquitoes that landed at the same time. "Where's our bug spray? These mosquitoes are bad."

"Hey, Ben," Rennen said, walking over to him. "What smells so good? I could smell it down at the beach."

"They're Indian tacos on fry bread. The smell is killing me. I'm so hungry I could eat it all! We can't eat until everyone is here."

"You don't have to wait any longer. We were the last ones here. Makenna could hardly paddle, and it slowed us way down," Rennen said.

"My sister, too. I thought we were going to tip over. I hope she doesn't want to paddle on the way back."

As they ate, three Calusa Indians told how their ancestors lived, caught fish with nets, and how they hollowed out cypress trees to make canoes.

"Coool," Ben said. He looked at the nearby trees and wondered what it would take to cut one down and hollow it out with just a knife. It must have taken a year!

After everyone finished eating, it was time to do the craft. The Indian women told how masks were made and at what ceremonies they were used. They showed the kids how they were made and invited them to make one for themselves.

Bekka created a festive mask—one worn during a celebration. Ben's mask was fierce looking, like a warrior. It would look great on his bedroom wall.

As the twins worked, several rangers walked up from the beach and talked to the ranger in charge. Ben and Bekka noticed and wondered what was going on. They wished they could get close enough to listen, but that wasn't possible. One ranger was moving his hands up and down but kept his voice down.

"Ranger Cory will take your masks back to the Visitor Center in his canoe just in case any of you should capsize," one of the Indians said as the last person finished. The photographer got a picture of everyone holding masks in front of their faces before the masks were put in a plastic tote.

"If you're finished, let's take off," Ben and Bekka's dad said. "Since this is our only day to be here, I want to head farther into the mangrove islands and do some exploring. Want to ask Rennen and Makenna to go with us?"

"Good idea," Ben said, heading off to find Rennen. Bekka got in a picture with the Calusa Indian women. She'd put it inside her mask as a reminder of where it came from.

Chapter 26

Ben and Rennen decided they wanted to ride together and headed for the Coopers' canoe.

"I'm sure the ride back to the Visitor Center won't be as terrifying as it was coming here," Ben said.

"I feel sorry for your dad with Bekka and Makenna in his canoe. If we hear anyone screaming, we'll know it's them."

"I heard that, Ben Cooper!" Bekka said, coming to get bug spray.

"Leave her alone, Ben," their father told him. "I'm sure they'll be just fine. She and Makenna are pretty brave compared to most ten-year-old girls."

"Yeah!" she shot back at her brother. Actually, she hoped they didn't encounter an alligator or a snake. She didn't feel all that brave. "Can I take your binoculars? Makenna and I both want a pair to watch for anhinga. I want to see one before we go home."

Bekka had seen pictures of the unusual big black birds, and thought binoculars would give her a better look at one if it was perched in a tree near the water.

"Okay, but don't get them wet," Ben instructed her.

"I won't. We're going to take our time going back so we can see everything. Makenna's dad said he would get pictures of us paddling."

"Just don't drown him," Ben said, running off with Rennen.

"Very funny!" Bekka said, wrinkling up her face.

Ben climbed on to the front seat of their canoe. It was agreed he would start out paddling and would trade places at the mangrove tunnel. The guys and Mr. Cooper put on their life jackets and shoved off from the shore. They were among the first ones to leave. Ben followed his father's directions about going around one island and then another. He was focused on paddling instead of what was around them.

"Ben, look, there's a manatee over there!" Rennen exclaimed. It was half swimming, half floating about twenty feet away. The ranger had told them they would probably spot one on the way back. Manatees are as big as hippos and the boys had wanted to see one.

Ben turned around to see where Rennen was pointing. He moved so quickly, the whole canoe rocked back and forth. He grabbed both sides of the canoe to steady it and dropped his paddle into the water.

"Oh no!" Ben exclaimed, reaching as far as he could with his right arm. He couldn't believe he had let go of his paddle.

"Can you get it, Ben?" his father asked. He was trying to steer the canoe over to where the paddle was drifting.

"I think so," Ben answered. He had to be careful because of the sawgrass in the water. He was within an inch or two of the paddle, wishing his arm was just a little longer. "Almost got it."

Behind him, Rennen was holding on to both sides of the canoe, leaning left to help keep it balanced. His eyes were almost popping out of his head. He knew how to swim and his life jacket would keep him up, but there were alligators, snakes, and now manatees in the water. Maybe he would have been safer with the girls.

"Ben, don't lean so far!" his father called to him. "Sit back down!" His voice got louder. "The canoe is going to flip!"

Too late! The weight of Ben's body made the canoe turn over and they found themselves in the Chokolaskee Bay.

Chapter 27

"Ben! Rennen!" Mr. Cooper called out to the boys as he came up out of the water.

Ben's head popped up, and then up came Rennen. Each boy spit out saltwater from their mouths and wiped their faces. They reached for the canoe which was floating upside down, but watched as their paddles floated away. Mr. Cooper tried to flip the canoe right side up, but couldn't.

"Boys, stay with the canoe, but be careful of the sawgrass," he warned, as he headed out in search of their paddles. The wind and current were taking them farther away.

Ben and Rennen looked around for signs of snakes or alligators. The ranger said manatees were gentle if they weren't frightened, so the boys tried to keep calm.

"Need some help, boys?" asked a man in a canoe who had paddled up behind them. Ben recognized them as part of their group.

"What happened?" asked one of his twins in astonishment. "Did a manatee flip your canoe over?"

Ben got red in the face. He wished it was something that dramatic. He didn't want to admit it was his mistake of reaching too far for a paddle. Rennen answered for him.

"I saw a manatee over there, so Ben looked to see it and dropped his paddle in the water, and he leaned too far, and tipped us over. His dad is way down there trying to get both of our paddles." Rennen pointed left, then right, then left again as he told the story.

"We'll stay with you until he gets back," the dad said. "Fortunately, the water's not over his head, so he can walk and get them."

And then the worst happened. The photographer from *Twins for Life* came around the bend with his camera in hand. He wanted to take a few pictures of wildlife in the water, but found something even better–two boys holding onto an upside down canoe. And no parent was in sight. He turned on his video camera

and asked, "What's your name, and what happened?" Then he recognized Ben. "Wait a minute, I know you."

Ben didn't want to talk to the reporter. He wanted to crawl under the canoe and hold his breath until his father came back.

"So what happened?" asked the photographer, looking from one boy to the other. "Remind me of your names. What happened to your sisters? You didn't leave them on the island, did you?"

"My name is Rennen and his sister is with my sister and Dad in our canoe. Ben was paddling up front and he dropped his paddle when he turned to look at a manatee. He reached too far and flipped our canoe. His Dad tried to turn it back over but couldn't, so he went after the paddles."

The photographer took a picture of them soaking wet. Ben wanted to swim away. He did not want this picture in the magazine, for sure! And then he heard a voice behind him that made him cringe.

"Hey, Ben, what happened?"

Ben couldn't believe his sister and Makenna had caught up to them.

"Where's Dad?" Makenna looked all around for their father.

For the third time, Rennen answered for Ben. "Your brother was paddling and looked over there to see a manatee and dropped his paddle in the water. He reached too far and flipped us over."

"Seriously, dude? You're the one who flipped it over?" Bekka asked, not believing what she was hearing. "But where's Dad?"

"He went after the paddles," Ben answered and pointed in the direction where they floated out of sight. "I wonder what's taking him so long."

Chapter 28

Makenna's father told the photographer that they would stay with the boys and their canoe if he would go find Mr. Cooper. While they waited, several other canoers came by and helped the boys turn their canoe back over. Ben and Rennen climbed in and sat there dripping wet, waiting for Mr. Cooper to return with the paddles. Bekka took pictures just to show their mother what really happened.

Within minutes, the two men came around the other side of the island paddling the canoe. They were laughing like they were best friends.

"Did you have to go very far to get the paddles?" Ben asked, relieved to see his father.

"Not too far. One got caught in cattails along the edge of an island, and the other we found down by another island. Ben, I do believe you're going to be mentioned in the magazine more than once."

"But that's not what I want people to read!"

The photographer got one last picture of Ben and Rennen. "I think I'll call this one, 'up a river without a paddle'."

Ben rolled his eyes and shook his head. What else could go wrong?

Mr. Cooper got out and climbed back into his own canoe. He thanked the photographer and the other men for their help. Rennen was in the front seat ready to take over paddling.

"Dad, before we go back, can we find a mangrove tunnel?" Bekka asked from the other canoe.

"Yes, if the others want to go see it. The ranger told me where one is," he said, paddling in the direction where he had just come from. The viney tunnel was in sight as they went around an island full of mangrove trees. It looked almost like a basket that was upside down in the water.

Bekka was paddling the other canoe and headed right for the tunnel. Just as she got near it, she screamed. She spotted two

bulging eyes looking at them from the tall grasses at the bank. "There's an alligator over there!"

"Where?" Makenna, Rennen, and Ben asked at the same time.

Bekka pointed with the paddle. "Over there!" She closed her eyes and ducked her head.

The alligator was just too close. She read alligators were fast swimmers and had a strong tail that could rock a canoe if it felt threatened.

"Bekka!" her father said sternly from his canoe. "Remain calm and keep paddling. Your scream probably woke him from his nap."

He took a deep breath himself. He couldn't believe he had been walking in that area not ten minutes before. "Paddle into the mangrove tunnel."

"But what if it follows us?" Bekka asked. She could hardly breathe. How could her father tell her to paddle past the alligator into the mangrove tunnel?

"It won't follow us. Keep going," her father assured her. Deep down inside, he was hoping the alligator wouldn't follow them.

Sitting in the middle seat, Makenna sat very calmly with her hands on her lap. She didn't want to hold the side of the canoe in case the alligator came by them. Makenna's father paddled harder since Bekka barely put her paddle into the water.

Chapter 29

The tunnel was like a maze of vines surrounding them. Green leaves growing on the mangrove trees created shade from the hot sun overhead. The water was calm and smooth. Just like her father said, the alligator hadn't followed them, so Bekka tried to relax.

"Wanna paddle, Makenna?" Bekka asked as they were at the end of the mangrove tunnel. She had had enough paddling for one day.

"Sure," Makenna said, "as long as that alligator doesn't follow us." She started to get up and move toward the front.

"Just a minute," Bekka said. "I want to take a picture of the mangrove tunnel." She turned and got a picture of their canoe leaving the tunnel behind.

Bekka's father laughed. He knew she was okay if she was back to taking pictures. In the distance they could hear the sound of a boat motor. It sounded like it was coming toward them going fast.

"Let's change now," Bekka said. She and Makenna stood up to change seats and were holding each other's arms when out of an inlet, a boat whizzed past them. The noise scared the girls causing them to fall back down into their seats. The waves almost tipped over their canoe.

"What was that?" Makenna screamed. She had never seen a flat-bottom boat with what looked to be a big round fan on the back.

"That's an airboat," her father replied. "The motor is up on the back so the propellers don't get caught in the sea grasses." His voice was drowned out by the roar of another boat.

"Watch out!" Ben yelled, seeing another boat coming from the same direction. The girls stayed down in the canoe as the motorboat sped by.

"That was a ranger's boat!" Mr. Cooper said. "Something's going on."

Waves from both boats rocked the two canoes so much, everyone was sure they were going to tip over. They sat perfectly still, holding onto the sides for balance. At last, things calmed down and all that was heard was the rustling of the wind in the tall grass.

"Can we go back now?" asked Makenna.

"No, let's stay out here longer," begged Ben. "That was cool. Let's try to follow them and see if the ranger catches the guy." He was pumped for adventure.

"Yeah!" said Rennen.

"If we do see them, don't do anything to attract attention to us," his father warned him and Ben.

Through the twists and turns around mangrove islands and another pass through a mangrove tunnel, they saw neither boat. Ben and Rennen were disappointed. They knew the man in the airboat was going faster than the speed limit for manatees.

"Bekka, if you're tired, you can come back over to our canoe and Rennen can paddle their canoe across the bay. Or do you girls think you can handle it?" her dad asked.

"We can handle it," Bekka said, looking at Makenna. "Girl Power, right?" She made fists with both hands and held up her arms.

"Right!" Makenna said, high-fiving Bekka. She picked up the paddle and moved to the front while Bekka climbed into the middle seat. They hoped the wind had calmed down to make it easy for them.

"You start, and we'll trade half way across," Bekka suggested.

"Okay. Let's go. Race ya, Rennen," Makenna said, challenging her brother who immediately put his paddle down deep into the water and pulled it back toward him.

"You think you can beat us? We'll show you!" he said, and off they went across the windy bay.

It was neck and neck as they paddled the two miles. With the wind at their backs, they felt like someone was pushing them to the shore. Halfway across, the twins changed seats and the other paddled. It was harder than it looked.

Chapter 30

Ranger Cory was at the dock to meet their canoes when they returned to the Gulf Coast Visitor Center. The boys threw up their arms in victory.

"Wait 'til you hear what happened to us," Bekka declared as the ranger grabbed the front end of their canoe.

"I have a feeling I know what you're going to tell me, and I would like all of you to meet in my office as soon as you turn in your paddles and life-jackets."

"Are we in trouble?" Makenna asked her father.

"I don't think so," he replied. "I don't think we did anything wrong other than upset a manatee and wake up an alligator with someone's screams."

"Da-ad," she said, poking him with her elbow.

"Mom! What are you doing here?" asked Bekka as they entered the building. Both she and Makenna and Rennen's mother were sitting on a bench near the door.

"A ranger was sent to pick us up," she said. "We're glad to see you're all right. I thought maybe something happened to you– like tipping over your canoe, and needing to be rescued."

"Well, we did sort of, but we don't know why they want to talk to us," her husband admitted.

"You tipped over your canoe?"

"Mom, it was the funniest thing," Bekka started to say but stopped when three rangers stepped toward them.

"Can you all please come into the conference room?" a ranger asked, opening the door to a room with a large table and twelve chairs. The rangers followed them.

"Thank you for being willing to meet with us. My name is Jim, this is Carol, and you know Cory. First of all, have you enjoyed your time here at the Everglades?" Ranger Jim asked.

Everyone answered with an enthusiastic, "Yes!"

"Good. I'm sure you'll have a lot to talk about when you get home, and lots of pictures to show people. And when *Twins for Life* magazine does its article on the triathlon, it will be much more interesting because your two families were here."

Ben and Bekka and Makenna and Rennen looked at each other and broke out laughing. Who would have guessed how their lives would be changed? They would never forget meeting each other. Or the dozens of mosquito bites they each had!

"We made some disturbing discoveries this week, and thanks to you kids, we think we're on to something," the ranger remarked. The four kids looked at each other and grinned.

Turning to Bekka he said, "The pictures you showed us yesterday were quite informative. Is it possible for us to look at others to see if you got any more of what we're looking for?"

"Wow!"

Chapter 31

Bekka was shocked that the rangers wanted to see her pictures. What were they looking for? she wondered. She looked at her parents who were nodding their heads yes.

"Sure," she said taking her camera from around her neck.

"We won't erase anything, we promise."

"Good, because I got some really good ones of Ben that I want to show his friends back home," she said, teasing her brother. She might not, but the look on his face was priceless.

Ranger Carol took Bekka's camera and left the room. In a few minutes she returned with a laptop computer. "I have a few pictures I want to ask you about."

The first one was at Shark Valley when Bekka took the picture of the man talking to the rangers who had his backpack. "Why'd you take this picture?"

Ben and Bekka looked at each other like they were busted, but Bekka answered, "We were getting pictures of a palm tree for the scavenger hunt. But actually, we thought he looked guilty of something, and since we seem to solve mysteries at national parks, we thought it would be good to have his picture. Was he stealing something in his backpack?"

Mrs. Cooper thought she was going to lose it. It sounded like her kids went looking for trouble after all, not that trouble came looking for them. What if that man had seen her taking his picture and came after her or the camera? She put her hand over her eyes and looked down.

The ranger was about to answer Bekka's question about the man's backpack but stopped himself.

Ranger Carol showed them another picture. She turned to Makenna and Rennen and asked, "See this man by the tree in the slough? Do you recognize him?"

Makenna and Rennen looked at it closely. "When. . .how did you get his picture?" Makenna asked Bekka.

Then they saw the snake in the water and remembered seeing Bekka take it over her shoulder as they left the slough. Both mothers gasped when they saw the snake's head.

"And today, I understand you had a bit of excitement in the waterway. Tell me about it." Everyone looked at Ranger Jim in surprise. He seemed to have eyes and ears all over the place.

"What part do you want to hear?" Mr. Cooper asked. "About us almost tipping over into the bay when another canoe ran into us, or when Bekka had us going in circles and almost tipped over because the wind was so strong, or when Ben flipped our canoe reaching for his paddle, or when I had to go wading around islands in sawgrass looking for the paddles, or Bekka flipping out when she saw an alligator, or when we almost got run down by a ranger's motorboat chasing an airboat at high speeds?"

"What?" Mrs. Cooper exclaimed, looking at each one of her family members. This was definitely the last national park they were ever going to visit.

The rangers broke out laughing. They had never heard of any family ever experiencing that much trouble in one day.

Ranger Jim narrowed it down for them. "It was the boat chase we are wondering about. By any chance did anyone get a picture of it or get a good look at the driver? He managed to get away, and we want to identify him and bring him in for questioning."

Trying as hard as they might, no one could think of much of anything to say since Makenna and Bekka were switching places and everyone was watching them as they fell. Except Mr. Cooper who was at the back of the two boats and had gotten a look at the man as he flew by in the boat.

"He had on a blue shirt. The reason I remember is that it was the same color of the sky, and he looked like his head and arms weren't attached. And then he was gone." The kids giggled.

"Does it look like this blue shirt?" Ranger Carol asked showing him the picture of the man in the slough.

"Yes, but it really stands out against the green algae and brown trees in this picture. What's going on?" Mr. Cooper asked.

"Give us one more day to work on this, and we might have an answer for you," Ranger Jim said. "Please don't mention any of this to anyone else. You never know who's in on this." Ranger

Carol gave Bekka her camera back after making a copy of Bekka's pictures–even the goofy ones of Ben.

Ranger Cory sat quietly trying to put all the pieces of the puzzle together. There had to be an answer.

The Coopers had many things to discuss on their way back to the campsite. First of all, Ben and Bekka had to calm down their mother and assure her they were never in great danger.

Chapter 32

"What else happened to you guys this afternoon?" the photographer asked Ben and Bekka that night as they sat down to eat hamburgers. They were the only group back at the campsite, and the cooks had the food ready to eat.

"I went around the island to get pictures of other canoers, and I never saw you again," the photographer said in between bites. "Anymore excitement after you got back into the canoe?"

The kids looked at each other and smirked.

"Our dad wanted to go see the mangrove tunnels, and it took us a long time to get back," Ben said, remembering the ranger's request not to mention anything to anyone.

"That sounds cool. Did you get pictures of everything for the scavenger hunt?" the photographer asked Bekka. "They're giving out awards tonight for those who got all of them."

"I forgot about the scavenger hunt," Bekka said, jumping up to go to the tent for her camera and Junior Ranger book. "I'll look to see what I still need pictures of."

As she walked back to the tent, she looked around at the campground and thought of the new friends they had made and the great times they had together. If she could have chosen any place to go for Spring Break, this would have been it. She learned

so much about Everglades National Park and wanted to come back someday.

It looked like someone down at a green tent was already packing to leave. She wondered why since the farewell wasn't until after breakfast in the morning. A man was loading bags into his Jeep. He looked her way and then turned away when he heard Ben yell to her.

"Come on, Bekka. What's taking so long?"

She couldn't answer, but hurried into their tent and sat down on her sleeping bag. She picked up her camera and looked at the pictures in the monitor. She had lots of pictures to look at, so it took her a few minutes. Was she seeing what she thought she was seeing?

"Come on, Bekka, what are you doing? Dad sent me over to see what is taking you so long," Ben said, stomping sand off his feet before going into the tent.

"Where are your binoculars?" she asked quietly and calmly.

"Right here. Why? What's up?" he asked as he reached for them under his pillow.

"Don't stick your head out–just use your binoculars and look through the doorway over to that green tent. What is that guy doing? Do you see anything funny?" Bekka instructed her brother.

"I don't see anybody. Wait a minute, he just came out. He's loading stuff into the Jeep. Oh, my gosh!" he said rather loudly.

Chapter 33

"Sh-h!" Bekka hissed at him. "Keep your voice down. He might hear you and leave."

"What are we going to do? How can we prove anything?" They had to think like two detectives.

"I don't know. We have to think, and think fast because he looks like he's leaving. But why? We aren't done with everything," Bekka said trying to come up with a reason and a quick plan.

"How about if we go over and tell him we know who he is?" Ben asked.

"No, that wouldn't work. I think the best thing is if we go back out and act as if we don't suspect anything. I'll take my camera, you take your binoculars, and we'll keep an eye on him. That'll give us time to think."

"Mom isn't going to like it when she hears what we're really doing," Ben said.

"But if we solve the mystery about who the thief is, she'll be happy," Bekka said picking up her camera and Junior Ranger book. "Let's go."

They tried not to look over at the green tent or act suspicious, and were relieved to see Ranger Cory and Ranger Allison drive into the campground parking lot. Another group of canoers came in right behind them. Their photographer took one last picture of

them together. Then everyone rushed to the food table to get their hamburgers.

"We seem to be missing the group who went to Ten Thousand Islands," Ranger Cory said. "While we wait for them to return, anybody have anything they'd like to tell us about their canoe trip? Was it harder or easier than you thought?"

"Harder," said one boy. "We kept hitting bottom with our canoe in the shallow water." They had been to the section where it was less than one foot deep.

Ben and Bekka and their friends looked at each other with surprise since they were in the bay where it was much deeper. Their canoe might not have tipped over if they had been in shallow water. But then they might not have seen the manatee, alligator, or almost been run down by two motorboats.

The noise of several car horns signaled that the last group had arrived. Caden, Camden, Tomas, and José piled out of their cars and came over to eat with Ben, Bekka, Makenna, and Rennen. Within minutes they were telling stories.

"We saw an alligator today," Ben said. "You should have seen the girls freak out. They didn't want to go anywhere near it."

"You should talk," Bekka shot back. "Who dropped his paddle and flipped his canoe?" Ben turned red and wished he hadn't said anything.

"That was nothing. You should have seen the rangers chasing a guy in an airboat. We don't know what happened, but the guy

got away from the ranger," Caden said. "Our dad said he was outside the national park waters, so no one could stop him. Maybe he was speeding or something."

As he talked, Ben, Bekka, Makenna, and Rennen just listened. They were sworn to secrecy and hoped the looks on their faces didn't give anything away. Could it be the same person the ranger was chasing near them? They weren't too far from the Ten Thousand Islands, so it could have been the same boats. It made them wonder.

"Did you get a picture of him?" asked Bekka.

"No. We tried to get our photographer to get one since he has that jumbo camera, but he said the guy was too far away. But we didn't think so," Tomas said, swatting at a mosquito on his forehead. No one would miss those pesky things after this week.

Bekka looked around the crowd. The photographer, who had just arrived, was asking a set of twins what they enjoyed doing the most and took their picture. He still had the bandages on his hand from being cut by sawgrass. Bekka wondered if it hurt much.

After the twins told the photographer they liked slogging in the slough best, he turned on his video camera and walked in a complete circle getting every part of the campground. Something caused him to jerk his camera in the other direction. Bekka knew why. She nudged Ben who was watching the man at the tent loading his sleeping bag, coolers, and other bags into the Jeep.

"Haven't we seen that before?" Ben asked.

"Yes, we have. When do you think we should talk to the rangers?" Bekka asked.

"Pretty soon."

"Hey, what're you two talking about so quietly?" asked Makenna.

"Not much," Bekka replied. She didn't want to tell what they suspected. She was relieved to see the ranger get up to talk.

"Is everyone done eating?" Ranger Cory asked, cupping his hands around his mouth. He stopped talking, hoping people would quiet down. Someone put their fingers to their lips and whistled loud enough for everyone to hear.

"Thank you," the ranger said, looking at the whistler. "If everyone is done, we'll clear the tables and give out some awards. I have certificates for those who completed the triathlon and patches for those who found everything on the scavenger hunt. Let's take a ten-minute break to clear the tables, and if you want to get your camera, please do so."

"Dad, we think we know something," Ben said to his father as he and Bekka walked with him to their tent for more bug spray. "We aren't sure exactly what and why, but we do know who."

"Really? What are you talking about?" he asked, proud that the twins had the instincts of a good reporter.

"I'll tell you in the tent." This was no time for an eavesdropper.

Chapter 34

Ben looked out the flap of their tent to see if anyone could hear him. No one was anywhere nearby.

"You know how you tell us to use our senses when we think something isn't quite right?" Ben asked. "Well, Bekka saw something, but we aren't sure how to get it out in the open."

Bekka took a few minutes to explain what they thought was happening in the green tent. Mr. Cooper was surprised, but with the strange things going on, he took it seriously.

Stepping out of the tent and barely looking at the green tent, he said quietly to the twins, "Let's talk to the rangers before the meeting begins. It's going to be dark soon, and we don't want anyone getting away with a crime."

Even though the meeting was about to begin, the rangers listened as Ben and Bekka told what they suspected, and watched what was happening at the tent. What the twins said made sense.

"If you're right, then you'll be heroes of Everglades National Park. But if you're not, then we'll be guilty of accusing people of things they didn't do," Ranger Allison said. With all her heart, she wanted them to be right.

"Let's call for back-up help," Ranger Cory said in case things got out of hand. He immediately placed a call to his partners, who

also thought the twins might be onto something. They told him they'd be there soon.

Looking at his watch, Ranger Cory blew his whistle to get the award ceremony started. All the participants and their parents sat quietly around the tables. Most everyone had cameras ready to take pictures.

"First of all, I'd like to thank *Twins for Life* magazine for sponsoring this triathlon," he stated. "It has been a great experience that none of you will ever forget."

Everyone clapped and cheered for the good time they had. Some wanted to return and do it all again.

"I'd like to thank the three photographers who came to do a story and take pictures for the summer issue. Would you men please stand so we can thank you with a round of applause?"

Two out of the three photographers stood. Cory asked if anyone had seen the third one named Rick.

"He said he was going to take a shower to rinse off the saltwater," one of the other photographers answered.

"When he comes out, I'd like a picture of the three of you with us rangers," Cory replied. "If anyone sees him, please let me know. Let's get on with the awards."

The ranger called the names of each twin since everyone had completed the fifteen-mile bike ride, the slog through the slough, and the canoe trip in the waterways. It was much more

than any of them ever imagined it would be. Parents clapped and clapped. It was a proud moment for them, too.

"I'd like to give special mention to some who seem to be outstanding for a number of reasons. Some of you were outstanding at finding ways to help preserve our park. It is endangered in many ways, and we hope all of you will help us keep it in good shape." He called the names of several twins and told what they did. More clapping and cheering.

The setting sun shone brightly in Ben and Bekka's faces as they looked at the green tent from time to time. They wondered what was going on inside. Two brown pickup trucks drove into the campground and went around to the campsites and stopped. Four men got out and stood by the trucks watching Ranger Cory give out awards. They saw him nod his head.

Chapter 35

Rick finally came out of the bathhouse and walked toward his tent. Ranger Cory called to him to go join the other two for a picture.

"Let me put my towel in my tent and grab my camera," he said.

Within a minute the photographer walked out of his tent carrying a camera bag. He took a minute to zip up his tent. Everyone understood. He didn't want mosquitoes in his tent either.

"Step over here with your two friends for a quick picture," Cory directed him. "This has been quite a week, and we want to remember your part in it." Rick set his bag down and went to stand by the other two photographers.

Several parents stood next to the ranger to get pictures of the men who had taken their pictures all week.

"How about if I get one of you three with your camera," Ranger Cory said, reaching for Rick's bag to get out his camera.

He opened the camera bag and jumped in surprise. His eyes did a double take. "What's this?" he asked. "Ranger Allison, can you please come over here?" Rick felt panic rising up from his stomach. He had grabbed the wrong camera bag by mistake.

Allison looked in the bag and gasped. Rick reached for it, but the ranger held on to it tightly. Cory nodded to the rangers by the truck and said, "I think it's time."

Two of the men moved toward the three photographers while two other rangers walked over to the green tent. Everyone turned to see what was happening. No one but the Coopers had any idea why the extra rangers were there.

One ranger went to the back end of the Jeep and looked inside the coolers. He gave Cory a nod then took it out and set it on the ground. The other ranger bent down to unzip the zipper.

"What are they doing?" asked Rick. His voice sounded angry.

"Just checking something out," answered Ranger Cory, holding out his arm. "Please, stay where you are."

The two other photographers stared at him, wondering what was going on. They had no idea. Ben and Bekka sat perfectly still. The hair on the back of their necks prickled. Their suspicions were correct. Something was not right.

Loud voices were heard coming from the tent. To everyone's shock, the two rangers stepped outside the tent holding the arms of another man. He tried to break away. Everyone gasped. They couldn't believe their eyes. Where did he come from? What was going on?

Chapter 36

The rangers walked the man over to where Rick stood by Ranger Cory. Everyone looked left, then right. Ben and Bekka's mother put her hand over her mouth hardly able to believe what she saw. The man was Rick's identical twin!

Ranger Jim took charge. "After seeing what these men had in their tent and Jeep, we need to ask them what they've been doing here in the Everglades. We would appreciate everyone's cooperation until it is settled."

Three rangers took the coolers and bags from Rick's Jeep and tent to search for more evidence. Allison held tightly to the camera bag as she got in a car.

No one could speak—not even the chatty girls. No one saw this coming and didn't know what to think. They could not believe one of the photographers was involved in a plot to do something wrong. Rick seemed like a good guy, getting pictures of everyone in Shark Valley, walking through the swamp at Big Cypress, and riding in a canoe around the Ten Thousand Islands. Why was his twin here? What had they been doing all week?

Ranger Cory walked to his car and came back with two grocery bags and an armload of skewers. He laid them on a picnic table and took a deep breath.

"Sorry, folks, but I need to leave, too. I need to be there when they question Rick and his brother about today's happening. Here are more fixings for s'mores. Enjoy another marshmallow roast under the stars. I'll be back in the morning to give out the rest of the awards." He hurried back to his car to catch up to the other rangers.

Little by little, people started talking, asking each other what they knew. No one guessed Ben and Bekka were the ones who alerted the ranger that something wasn't right. To keep from having to answer questions, their parents went to the food table to open the marshmallows and candy bars,

"Let's get a fire going and make some s'mores," Mr. Cooper suggested. "Time to enjoy our last night in the Everglades."

"Sounds good to me," Caden and Camden's grandfather said. "We're going back to Iowa where it's cold."

"And we have to go back to school," Ben stated. That brought on a round of groans from all the twins. No one liked that thought.

Sparks from a roaring fire blew upward in the dark sky as the smell of roasting marshmallows filled the air. Constellations were easy to find in the night sky with the park being so dark. Some twins had never spotted anything other than the Big Dipper and got excited when someone pointed to Orion.

"Who knew our trip to the Everglades would end with suspense?" Rennen and Makenna's mother said.

"I could have told you it would," replied Mrs. Cooper.

"Really?"

"Really. My children are magnets for trouble when we visit national parks. It never fails. And with all these twins, I could have predicted there would be double trouble in the Everglades."

As they roasted marshmallows for a second s'more, Bekka and Ben laughed. It was true. They were magnets for trouble. Even way down in Everglades National Park.

Chapter 37

"Ben, get up," Bekka said, shaking his sleeping bag the next morning. "The rangers are here already."

"What?" he asked, sticking his head out of the sleeping bag.

"The rangers are here and breakfast is almost ready," Bekka said, tying her clean tennis shoes. Their mother refused to let them bring the ones they wore to the Cypress slough into the tent. They were still green with algae and they stunk. She was ready to recycle them.

No one was late getting to breakfast. Everyone wanted to hear what the rangers had to say. No one dared say anything about it; instead they talked about the triathlon and the great time they had. Some exchanged phone numbers and email addresses to keep in touch. Some thought they might come back to the Everglades some day.

"In five minutes we'll start the award ceremony again," Ranger Cory announced as he walked from table to table. This was one triathlon he'd remember for a long time, in more ways than one.

"Sit by me," Makenna said to Bekka as they disposed of their breakfast plates and cups. "Are you and Ben going to get a special award because you helped solve the mystery?"

"What mystery?" Bekka asked. She tried to keep a straight face.

"You know. The mystery of the camera bag. What do you think is in the camera bag?" Makenna asked, hoping for information.

"I don't know. Really!" Bekka said. She was just as curious as everyone else.

Another ranger stood up to talk. "Good morning, my name is Jim. I'm the head ranger here at Everglades National Park. I hope you've had a great time while here."

Everyone clapped, whistled and yelled, "We did!"

"I'm sure you want to hear about what happened last night, so I'll tell you what I know." No one moved or said anything. They wanted to hear every word.

"The situation was as much a surprise to us as it was to you. We observed things happening this week, but they didn't seem to fit together. On Monday an individual was caught removing baby turtles. He was fined and had to leave the park."

Bekka looked at Ben and nodded her head. "That was the guy who passed us on the bike at Shark Valley."

They looked back at the ranger who said, "On Tuesday, while you were slogging in the slough, one of our groups encountered a man at a hardwood hammock."

Ben and Bekka looked at Rennen and Makenna, who looked at Caden and Camden, who looked at Tomas and José. They really were in the middle of a plot.

Ranger Jim continued, "Someone was stealing liguus snails off trees. As you know, removing anything from a national park is against our rules. Ranger Allison was more than distressed when she found a number of them missing, but no one was seen doing it." He looked at the crowd and noticed everyone was listening to his every word.

"Yesterday was a great day for canoeing. Everyone enjoyed themselves, but a couple of our families had a near miss by an individual in an airboat that was speeding. Much to our dismay, he got away from our rangers who were in pursuit, and took off up the coast."

These events were news to almost everyone. Some of the boys whispered they wished it had happened to them. Others said they saw the chase out in the islands.

"We didn't think there was a connection until someone noticed something and came to talk to us," the ranger stated. People looked around, trying to guess who it might be.

Makenna touched Bekka's arm. "It's you. I know it's you," she whispered. Bekka smiled and looked straight at the ranger. She wanted to hear the whole story.

Chapter 38

Taking a deep breath, the ranger told what happened with Rick and his twin.

"Late last night, I called *Twins for Life* magazine to ask about Rick's job as a photographer. They were surprised to hear he had a twin brother, named Mick, and shocked to hear he was involved in a crime.

"As you might have observed at Big Cypress Preserve, Rick went from group to group taking pictures. In between groups he went to the hardwood hammocks and snatched several liguus tree snails without being detected. Ranger Allison was shocked when someone pointed out some snail shells were missing. She had no idea a photographer was the guilty party."

Bekka looked around at the crowd. Some were nodding their heads and agreeing that they remembered seeing Rick there.

"What did Rick do with them?" someone asked.

"He hid them in his camera bag that he carried on his back. Going undetected, Mick, Rick's brother hid behind trees until groups left, and then they put the snails in a camouflage bag which Mick took with him. One of our groups talked to him, but didn't recognize him with his sunglasses and hat on."

Shocked, Ben and Bekka jerked their heads to look at each other—their eyes popped open. Then they looked at the other six

friends who did the same. Who knew they were in the middle of a crime spree?

"Rick carried them in the camera bag that he picked up by mistake last night. Many thanks to a person whose pictures helped put the puzzle pieces together."

Makenna elbowed Bekka and said, "You, I bet it's you he's talking about!" Bekka raised her eyebrows and smiled, just a little bit, as the ranger kept talking.

"Yesterday's canoe trip won't be soon forgotten by that same group of twins. After questioning him last night and doing a little investigating, we discovered Mick was fishing without a license. It was him the rangers were chasing in the airboat. The cooler we found in Rick's Jeep wasn't filled with hot dogs and soft drinks, but a dozen foot-long garfish. He planned to sell them to an aquarium in Orlando. Fortunately, the fish were still alive so we released them back into the bay."

Many cheered and whistled that the fish were still alive and back in the Everglades waterway.

Picking up his stack of awards, Ranger Jim said, "That's all we know now, so let's get on with handing out the rest of the awards. We hope your experiences of the triathlon will live long in your memories, and these certificates of commendation will hang somewhere in your home for all to read."

As Ranger Cory called out names, twins came forward to receive their awards. Smiles filled their faces. Much to their

disappointment, Ben and Bekka did not get one for the scavenger hunt. No matter how hard they looked, they did not see a raccoon or a turkey vulture. They would see them back in Michigan. They cheered for those who did find everything.

"We would like to give out a couple of special awards for a set of twins whose keen eyes and quick thinking broke open the case of the missing liguus snails. You're probably wondering who they are, and how they figured it out." Many in the crowd nodded their heads yes, and looked around.

"Bekka and Ben Cooper, please stand," the ranger said, pointing to where they sat. Looking surprised, the twins stood.

Walking over to their table, the ranger continued. "You might have noticed, Bekka has a camera and uses it all the time while Ben has binoculars which he likes to use.

"Yesterday after dinner, Bekka was in their tent and observed a man walking back and forth from his tent to his Jeep. He looked like Rick. But she knew Rick was the one who was cut on the sawgrass and had a large bandage wrapped around his hand. She also knew he was the photographer for the group who hadn't returned from the canoe trip.

"She got suspicious when she saw the person in the tent loading things into the Jeep. She asked Ben to use his binoculars to get a good look at him and what he was doing." The ranger stopped and looked around. He had everyone's attention.

"The man didn't have a bandage on his hand, and he was wearing the same blue shirt the kids said the man was wearing in

the swamp. And he looked just like Rick. That's when they knew they were on to something and had to report it.

"No one was more surprised to see Mick in the tent than Rick when he went to take a shower. Mick wasn't supposed to come until after dark to help pack."

Turning again to Ben and Bekka, he said, "Thanks to you two, Mick and Rick won't be back to steal anymore snails or fish, and our park won't be as endangered." People clapped, cheered and whistled for the young heroes.

"Wow!" Ben exclaimed. His face suddenly got a bright shade of red.

Ranger Allison came forward holding two gift bags. She set one down on the table and held up the second bag. "Bekka, because of the pictures you showed us of the suspect in the Cypress slough, we want to give you the Golden Camera award."

The ranger pulled out an old camera that had been spray painted gold and handed it to Bekka. It would make a fun souvenir. As the crowd clapped, Makenna took a picture of Bekka with her own camera.

Next, Allison walked over to Ben and said, "Ben, this is your lucky day. In honor of your needing a ranger to rescue your bike from the canal while an alligator and her baby watched, for coming in last at the bike ride, for turning green in an algae ball fight, unbelievably flipping your canoe, and not knowing the difference between an apple snail and a snail kite, I am pleased to present to

you the very first Everglades National Park Liggy Snail Award."

Allison reached into the bag and pulled out a slime-green plastic snail shell. Turning many shades of red, Ben blushed as people cheered.

"Hey, Ben, smile!" a photographer said, snapping a picture. "This is your lucky day. You made it into the magazine."

Ben groaned as he accepted the award. "But this is not what I want to be famous for."

THE END

BEKKA'S F.Y.I. (FOR YOUR INFORMATION)

TRAVELING TO FLORIDA

Ben and Bekka's family traveled 1500 miles from Lansing, MI to the Everglades National Park. How far would you travel?

Everglades
National Park

DID YOU KNOW?

1. Florida is called the Sunshine State?

2. The State bird is the Northern Mockingbird?

3. The State animal is the Florida Panther?

4. The State flower is the Orange Blossom?

5. The Atlantic Ocean is on the East coast while the Gulf of Mexico borders the west coast?

6. Almost twenty million people live in Florida?

7. Florida is 846 miles long from the Georgia border at the north to Key West at the southern end

8. Calusa Indians lived in the Everglades area for thousands of years, but disappeared in the late 1700s?

9. Miccosukee and Seminole Indians now live in Florida?

10. There are about one million alligators and thousands of pythons in Florida?

FACTS ABOUT EVERGLADES NATIONAL PARK

1. Ernest F. Coe saw the tropical beauty in south Florida and worked hard for it to become a national park. He became known as the *Father of the Everglades*.

2. Marjory Stoneman Douglas wrote "The Everglades: River of Grass", and agreed the Everglades should be protected as a national park.

3. Everglades became a National Park in 1947.

4. Due to people changing the flow of fresh water into south Florida, Everglades National Park is endangered because of the rising ocean level.

5. Everglades National Park is part of the largest wetlands ecosystem in the USA.

6. 366 species of birds including anhinga, white pelican, blue heron, roseate spoonbill, white isis, wood stork, snail kite, osprey, and flamingos soar above the sea of grass.

7. 50 species of reptiles, including 27 kinds of snakes, 16 species of turtles, and 15 species of amphibians are found in the park.

8. 40 specials of mammals, including the bobcat, manatee, Florida panther and armadillo call Everglades their home.

9. The only place on earth where alligators and crocodiles live in the same habitat is Everglades National Park.

10. Liguus Tree Snails have 3 to 5 narrow bands of colorful stripes. Fifty-nine color combinations have been found.

11. There is a Triathlon at Everglades National Park – ride a bicycle 15 miles at Shark Valley, paddle a canoe 4 miles out to and around Sandfly Island, and slog 3 miles in the Shark River swamp (slough) at Big Cypress Preserve.

GLOSSARY OF WORDS HEARD AT EVERGLADES NATIONAL PARK

1. Seagrass – seven types of tall grass found in the "river of grass".

2. Sawtooth Seagrass – a plant with saw tooth edges that can cut skin. Apple snails lay eggs at the base of the plant.

3. Brackish water – the water where the salty ocean water meets fresh river water. It is two-thirds salt water.

4. Cypress knees – extensions of the Cypress tree which stands in fresh water. Air plants grow on its smooth bark.

5. Mangrove – vine-like tree found in fresh or salt water.

6. Mangrove tunnel – vine-like trees standing in water form a tunnel through which you can canoe.

7. Hardwood Hammock – a high and dry island of trees which is above the level of the water.

8. Gumbo Limbo tree – red bark tree found on hardwood hammocks.

9. Liguus Snails – snails with colorful shells. They hibernate on the smooth bark of trees like the Gumbo Limbo.

10. Snail Kite – a predator hawk which eats only apple snails.

11. White pelican – the largest bird, standing 6 feet tall with wing spans of eight to nine feet.

12. Alligators – green reptiles with two layers of eyelids to see underwater, have a pointed snout, and can grow to 12 feet long.

13. American Crocodiles – brown reptiles, have a rounded snout, can grow up to 13 feet long, and are endangered.

14. Manatee – called a sea cow and can weigh up to 3,500 pounds. Many are injured by boat engine propellers.

15. Roseate Spoonbills – get their orange color from eating coral crustaceans. Their curved beaks peck for insects.

16. Anhinga – Black bird with a long neck, sharply pointed bill, and webbed feet.

17. Burmese python – one of many alien snakes that have been released in the Everglades endangering animals.

18. Ecosystem – The interaction of all living things with water, air, and minerals.

CAMPING RECIPES

CALUSA INDIAN FRY BREAD

In a bowl, mix together 2 cups of flour with 3 teaspoons
of baking powder and 1 teaspoon of salt. To this add
1 cup of milk and stir. Add a little more flour until the
dough does not stick to your hands when you mix it.

Form a ball the size of a lemon. On a floured surface,
roll it out to the size of a plate. Put it in a pan with hot oil.
Fry until it is golden. Flip and cook the other side.
Drain extra oil off. Add meat and other toppings.
Fold over like a taco and enjoy.

S'MORES

Place 2 marshmallows on a skewer or a long stick
and roast over a campfire.

When they are golden brown, remove
and put on one half of a graham cracker.

Layer one half of a flat chocolate bar on top
and add the other graham cracker.

WILDLIFE IN THE EVERGLADES

Visitors to Everglades National Park could see these mammals and reptiles.

American Crocodile

Brown pelican

Manatee

Spoonbill Roseate

Snail Kite

Burmese Python

Indigo Snake

Anhinga

American Alligator

Blue Heron

Liguus Snail

Florida Panther

MEET THE CHARACTERS

Hannah and Ethan Hopewell as Bekka and Ben Cooper

Real twins Tom and Joe Haynie as Tomas and José

Makenna and Rennen Morgan as themselves

WHICH DIRECTION ARE BEN AND BEKKA GOING NEXT?

A	B	C	D	E	F	G	H	I
⇨	⇦	⇨	⇦	⇨	←	→	↑	↓

J	K	L	M	N	O	P	Q	R
↖	↗	↙	↘	↔	↕	▲	▼	△

S	T	U	V	W	X	Y	Z
▽	◀	▶	◁	▷	◣	◢	◥

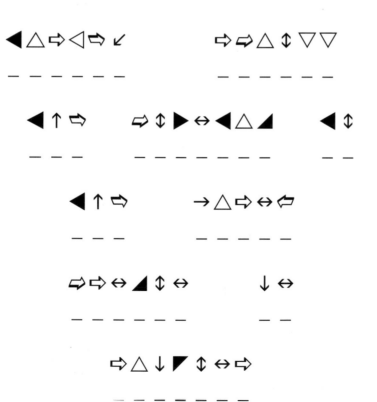